THE PRESIDENT'S REPRESENTATIVE BEGAN . . .

"Two days ago the President sent for me. He'd just had a top-secret message from Moscow on the hotline. Soviet Intelligence claims that the CIA in Teheran is planning a nice little revolution. They're going to assassinate the Shah and replace him with one of their own men."

"So what do you want me to do about it?" Malko asked.

"Go to Teheran."

"Where I do what? Ask the CIA chief—in the nicest possible way—whether he's planning to assassinate the Shah and fix me for an encore?"

"No, you have a cover story. The CIA in Teheran is low on secret funds at the moment. As you know, aid to underdeveloped countries doesn't always get there via the bank . . . It's kind of tricky, sending six hundred thousand dollars by cable."

"And who's to be the lucky recipient of these six hundred thousand iron men?"

"The chief of the CIA, General Schalberg."

"That's nice. That's what I call a visiting card."

"And when you've delivered you can have a week's holiday in Iran . . ."

The Malko Series

MALKO
VERSUS THE CIA

by
Gerard de Villiers

Translated from the French
by Adrian Shire
Revised English Translation
by Gerard de Villiers

PINNACLE BOOKS • NEW YORK CITY

MALKO: VERSUS THE C.I.A.

First published in French under the title *S.A.S. contre C.I.A.*
© Librairie Plon, 1965.

Published in England under the title *SAS Versus the CIA* by New English Library Limited.

Revised English translation © 1974 by Gerard de Villiers.

A Pinnacle Book, published by special arrangement with Librairie Plon and Gerard de Villiers.

ISBN: 0-523-00316-1

First printing, March 1974

Printed in the United States of America

PINNACLE BOOKS, INC.
275 Madison Avenue
New York, N.Y. 10016

CHAPTER ONE

Throat-stinging smell of burning kerosene. Past one in the morning and the cement of the airfield still soaked with heat. The little blue lights outlining the runways gave the landscape a modern feeling. Malko Linge noticed that each bulb stood beside a gas lamp, and smiled silently. Teheran's electricity supply has a will of its own.

The huge 747 rolled to a halt near the main airport building. There were only a few other planes; an Air India Boeing, an SAS Coronado, and a few antique Dakotas carrying the markings of various disreputable Middle Eastern lines.

The passengers trailed submissively away in the wake of a cheerfully plump black stewardess.

Malko gazed round.

No one seemed to be waiting. "Somebody," they had said, would meet him at the airport. The observation balcony was deserted. The big luminous clock said ten past one. In New York it was four fifteen, Malko thought wearily. He should have stayed in his house at Poughkeepsie, instead of coming to this country of the damned where gas vapors seemed to be the principal component of the atmosphere.

The other passengers were lining up at two glass cubicles, inside which a pair of sleepy, unshaven officials pored mysteriously—or in mystification— over the foreign passports. Malko's own was diplomatic; that meant he didn't have to get in line. A tiny Iranian, his teeth flashing below an enormous mustache, saw Malko's title and blinked. He was obviously dying to ask what a Serenissime Highness was but did not dare.

Prince Malko Linge was Austrian by birth, despite his American diplomatic passport, and the title was his by right. He was proud of it, as proud as he was of the castle in Austria. He intended to restore that castle and spend the rest of his life there, after the money he'd earned in his somewhat special work for the American government enabled him to do so. He had a contract with the CIA. He was a counterspy.

"Do you need a car?" the official asked politely.

"Thank you, a taxi will be fine."

Malko again looked round the customs hall at the first arrivals surrounding him. Fifty Iranians pressed up against a glass wall, trying to see the passengers.

The baggage arrived. The potbellied customs man stuck a label on each one and smiled meaningfully at Malko. Malko smiled back, and gave him a five-rial note.

Still no one came. Schalberg knew he was coming; even the plane was on time. Malko took a firmer grip on the handle of the black briefcase, as if the leather were transparent and the contents visible. He had thought of chaining it to his wrist, but that would have been absurd. It would also have been advertising. He'd be damn glad when he'd handed the thing over to Schalberg.

A ragged porter took his cases, and he followed, suffocating. Though the airport was five thousand feet up the heat was intolerable. Teheran is like a furnace in June.

Sweat trickled down his back. He realized with disgust that his black alpaca suit must be completely crumpled. He loathed untidiness.

Malko slid his hand inside his jacket and adjusted the butt of his special, superflat pistol in his waistband. That was the most discreet place for it,

6

but in the heat the metal stuck unpleasantly to his skin.

Standing on the pavement in front of the airport building, he stopped. There was a bar on the first floor, but he'd have to climb that long marble staircase. It was too far. Better go straight to the hotel; they would have a safe, and he would have all the time he needed for the absorption of healing vodka and lime.

There were several taxis in the rank. He put his hand up to call one, when a voice behind him said:

"Are you lost?"

He recognized the charming, slightly singsong accent of the little German stewardess who had looked after him on the flight from Paris. He turned around. She was holding a bag in one hand and a coat in a plastic cover in the other.

"Er—not exactly. I was trying to decide which of those cab-drivers had the fewest criminal tendencies."

She smiled.

"Why don't you ride with us in the Pan Am bus? The captain won't mind, he's a friend of mine."

For a moment Malko hesitated. Perhaps whoever was to have met him was late. On the other hand Hildegarde (she had told him her name on the plane) did have a very nice figure. They had been talking in German; now the conversation would be taken a step further in the Hilton bar. It is well known that women are more vulnerable when they are abroad. And his briefcase would be at least as safe surrounded by the Pan Am flight crew as it would be between a couple of Persian bodyguards of doubtful integrity. In Iran, integrity is always dubious when anything over a dollar is involved.

"Okay," he said. "Lead on."

He took a last look around, and then climbed into the VW Microbus waiting by the curb.

Hildegarde sat next to him, making no attempt

7

to conceal her interest. He smiled to himself, wondering what she would do if she knew just what it was that she was protecting.

He winced as the barrel of the pistol dug into his thigh.

"Is this your first trip to Teheran?" she was asking.

"No, I was here during the war. It wasn't much fun. I hope the hotels are a bit more comfortable."

"The Hilton's the best. You'd hardly believe the others. The night switchboard-operator of the Park Hotel speaks no language known to man ... Will you be staying long?"

"About a month. I have to visit a couple of places, I'm looking for a site for a nitrates factory. In the Persian Gulf, I expect. But I'll have plenty of free time."

"I s'pose you've got all your business papers in that briefcase?"

Malko smiled. Some papers.

"Oh, they're absolutely vital. That's why they never leave my side."

Hildegarde smiled. She put her hand on Malko's right hip, and in a natural voice asked:

"And is this papers too?"

She had her hand on the butt of the pistol. She had spoken in German, and no one took any notice. Malko bit his lip. He shouldn't have broken his rule. This was a lousy time to attract attention, he'd have to come up with a good story.

"Well, you know, the roads aren't always safe in this sort of country, and I have to go to some pretty wild places."

Hildegarde, laughing a little, said:

"Still, the road from Mehrabad to Teheran ...

"You're a smuggler?" she suggested "What're you carrying? Diamonds, emeralds? Not drugs, I hope."

Malko shook his head.

8

"No, I promise it isn't drugs."

"I believe you. You don't look that bad. But what is it?"

"I can't tell you. Not right now."

Not right now. Not ever. Only the President of the United States, the head of the CIA Middle-Eastern sector and Malko himself knew about this one. And the "others." But they wouldn't say anything.

"Promise me you won't tell anyone else what you're thinking," demanded Malko. "Please, it's very important."

He stared into her eyes, his own irises gleaming golden. No woman could resist that gaze. It was liquid gold. But this time he was not using it to get Hildegarde into bed. Not yet, anyway. For the moment he was playing for bigger stakes.

"Okay. But you're going to have to take me out tomorrow. I don't want you disappearing."

"I promise. Anyway, we're staying at the same hotel."

The little bus had reached the suburbs of Teheran. The great Avenue Shah Reza was flooded with yellow sodium light. Not a dog to be seen. The only moving things were a few late taxis, lit from inside with multicolored garlands of tiny lights.

The other passengers dozed. In the darkness, Malko took Hildegarde's hand and gently squeezed it. Instead of drawing back, she moved closer to him.

On his other side the captain grunted softly. Malko put his briefcase down beside the captain's, and moved his legs across to press against Hildegarde's.

The Volkswagen turned into the Avenue Hafez, and started the painful climb toward the Hilton, which is in the Chimeran quarter, about four miles outside the town.

There were very few houses now. The road

wound between bare hills, pegged with occasional buildings.

Malko, too, was getting sleepy. Everything was going very well. Soon he would be in the hotel, in the cool. The briefcase would be locked up in the manager's safe, and five dollars slipped to the porter would ensure that he had a room next to Hildegarde's.

The bus braked hard.

Malko woke up and stared out of the window, leaning on Hildegarde's shoulder. The vehicle rolled gently forward, then stopped on the verge. The door was jerked open, and a face appeared, visible beneath a cap. An Iranian, with a tiny Valentino mustache and bloodshot eyes, brandishing an enormous pistol.

"Everybody out!" he shouted. "Military control!"

The captain woke with a start. "What's all this shit?" he shouted furiously. "Nobody stops us. Come on, driver, get going!"

But the driver had a machine-gun pointed at his belly and a family at home. He muttered something incomprehensible, and didn't move.

The Iranian officer grabbed the steward roughly by the arm and forced him outside.

"Everybody out!" he insisted.

This time no one needed a second telling. Even the captain got up, perhaps impressed by the uniform. This stinks, thought Malko. A control like this in the middle of the night was on the bizarre side. He had an idea; it took a moment's work . . .

It was his turn to climb down; Hildegarde followed. The officer saw him, and snapped: "Who are you? Are you a civilian? What you doing hiding in the crew's bus? Where are your papers?"

Malko handed over his passport. In his other hand was the briefcase. But the officer was hardly looking at him. He turned and called to two men in plain clothes who had been standing in the shadow.

"Take this one," he shouted in Persian. Then, in English, for the benefit of the other passengers:

"You can go. We are holding this gentleman on suspicion."

Still half asleep, they got back into the bus. Hildegarde was last. She turned as she climbed in and shot Malko an anxious glance. He winked at her reassuringly. He hoped that she had seen it in the darkness.

The two men that the officer had called hemmed him in on either side. They took Malko by the arms and dragged him toward an old American car parked a little way away. The six soldiers placidly lowered their submachine guns and waited. As he passed them Malko heard one say in Persian: "Lieutenant Tabriz said we could turn in after this."

Malko gave no sign that he had understood. Details like that can sometimes save one's life. He offered no resistance as they hustled him into the car, wondering whether the game would end with anything more than just a one-way ride in the desert . . .

One of the men searched him and took away the pistol. Then they got into the car. Malko hung on to his briefcase.

Another man in plain clothes was at the wheel. He let in the clutch at once.

"Where are we going?" Malko asked, in English, to keep up his front.

No answer. The car quickly left the highway and took a side-road, bouncing over the uneven ground. It occurred to Malko that the Pan Am captain would not be able to warn anyone in time.

He still clutched the briefcase like a precious possession. The car suddenly slowed down and stopped. The man on his left opened the door and pulled him out.

As he had expected. A wasteland. In the distance twinkled the lights of Teheran. Malko tensed his

11

muscles; he would have to make a break for the darkness. But they gave him no time to jump. One grabbed him from behind, pinning his arms. He was enormously strong. Malko could not breathe. The other man took his wrist in one hand and the case in the other. He placed his foot in Malko's gut and pulled as hard as he could.

Malko gasped and let go the briefcase. Immediately the man who had been holding him let him go. A violent blow caught Malko behind the ear. He crumpled on to the stony, still-warm ground.

He dimly heard the car start up and turn around. He was alone. They had not dared, or wished, to kill him.

He struggled to his feet, and threw up. That was the foot in his belly. The sky was full of stars. The heat of the day lingered on. A dog barked a long, long way away.

He started to walk along the road that the car had taken. At least, he thought, the incredible story that he had been told in Washington was not a figment of General Gavin's sick mind.

Twenty minutes later he was back on the main road. Not unsurprisingly there was no sign of either the officer or the soldiers. Now all he had to do was get back to the Hilton.

He stood by the side of the road for nearly half an hour. A few cars passed, but they were all private, or taxis carrying fares. Eventually an empty taxi came down the hill. Malko stopped it. The driver was reluctant to go back into town; he was going home to bed; still, for 400 rials he would turn around. It was a 60-rial ride, but this was scarcely the time to make an issue of it.

His head ached like hell, and a trickle of blood had dried along his cheek. The taxi stopped in front of the Hilton; the doorman was asleep, so Malko went straight into the lobby.

The airline captain was standing, bare-headed and waving his arms, in the middle of a group of people including several civilians and an Iranian in uniform.

The Iranian saw him first. He shouted, and they all turned around. The captain rushed across.

"Christ we were worried about you. I thought those bastards had rubbed you out. You know those apes pay for their gear with our good dollars!"

The Iranian started: "I cannot allow you to . . ."

"Shut up, you shit," the American interrupted, "or I'll kick you right out of here. You'd better find the lunatic who let this happen."

The officer lifted his hands toward the sky in a gesture of helplessness.

"I'll write a report; but where do you suggest I look for them? I don't understand this at all."

Malko's head was spinning again. He looked around, looking for somewhere to sit down. Then he caught sight of Hildegarde, asleep on one of the sofas, and felt a sudden small glow of pleasure. Clutched in her hands was a black leather briefcase. *His* briefcase. . . .

Telepathically, the captain turned to him again and said: "What happened to my case? Did they take it? I guess they thought there was money in it."

Then he got very angry; he turned on the Persian and carefully explained: "Without my briefcase, which contains all the aircraft's papers, my plane will not be able to take off tomorrow morning. If it can't take off, you'll get a bill for a hundred thousand bucks, and that'll just be the beginning. My company will sue your country!"

A horrified silence descended on his hearers. The second secretary of the American embassy stood helplessly around, still half-asleep and completely dumbfounded by the idea of the Iranian army attacking a Pan Am bus. A dignified English gentleman turned out to be the manager of the Hilton; he, too, had been awakened in a hurry, and had not

13

had time to put on a tie (he felt completely undressed). The Iranian officer had been sent for by the manager. He had no idea what was going on, and clearly would rather not take the lead.

Since there seemed to be no likelihood of his getting back his briefcase, the captain let himself be persuaded to go to bed. But from his expression one might assume that the morning would be a difficult one.

He had in fact roused the hotel, not for Malko, but for his precious briefcase, which Malko had just had time to switch with his own as he got out of the bus. Nothing looks quite so like a black briefcase as another. Even the American had only spotted the difference when he had come to open it, and discovered that it was locked.

Malko looked tenderly down at Hildegarde. He shook her gently. She started, and opened her eyes.

"God, you're hurt!" she exclaimed, seeing the dried blood on his face.

"No, no, it's nothing. But I have to thank you. You were perfect; no one suspected anything."

"I'm glad you're happy; because now there's something you can do for me."

"Which is?"

"Open the briefcase. I want to know what's in it that's so important."

"I'm sorry, that's quite impossible."

"I suppose you'd rather I told the captain you had a gun. *He'd* make you open it."

She had him there.

"Right. Okay. But not down here. Meet me in my room."

"Make sure you don't lock yourself in or anything. In fact maybe you'd better come to my room. It's number 716."

"All right," Malko said. "I've never turned down an invitation to a lady's room."

14

CHAPTER TWO

Hildegarde's room faced south. Beyond the window, closed on account of the air-conditioning, the whole of Teheran lay spread-eagled. The Hilton's twenty-story bulk rose straight out of the empty desert, on the slopes of Elbrouz.

Malko knocked softly on her door.

It opened at once. She had exchanged her uniform for a short flowered nightdress. She had pretty legs, and Malko could see her nipples through the thin material.

"Quick, come in," she smiled, "you'll ruin my reputation."

Malko did not need telling twice; he went in and threw the briefcase on the bed. His own room was on the same floor, but he hadn't had time to take a shower. He was exhausted, and his wound had started to bleed again.

"Still interested?"

"Still. May I open it?"

"You must understand that once it's open, your life will be in danger."

She gave a little shiver.

"That's just too bad. This kind of thing never happened to me before, and I'm sick of airplanes, and I'm sick of fetching drinks for men who want to sleep with me."

"Okay. Here, open it."

He took a flat key from his pocket and held it out to her.

The lock made a small, sharp noise. Hildegarde

15

tugged at the strap and with a quick movement opened the case over the bed.

"Oh."

She didn't move.

A heap of packets of hundred-dollar bills spread over the bedspread, not much more than you would need to buy the Empire State Building. She looked dazedly at Malko.

"But ... but ... how ... how much?"

"Six hundred thousand," Malko said casually.

"What's it all for? Did you steal it?"

"No I did not."

"So?"

"So I can't say any more. You wanted to know what was inside; now you know."

"What are you going to buy with all that money?"

"Consciences."

"You should be able to afford quite a few."

"Not necessarily. The higher up they are, the more they cost. Poor guys, you don't buy."

"Why not?"

"Cheaper to kill them."

"I ... You're completely inhuman."

"I don't think so. Now, isn't it time we got to bed?"

"What?"

"Listen, you're going to help me. You wanted some excitement, now you're getting it. The gang that tried to grab the cash this evening aren't going to give up now, and they've only got until tomorrow morning. But I didn't trust the hotel safe, and I don't have a gun any more. They won't come looking for me here—at least I hope not."

"But where are you going to sleep? There's only one bed."

"The way my head is now there won't be any funny business, and in any case I'm completely knocked out. Now, is it yes or no?"

She hesitated. "Yes."

16

"Great. Now give me a hand."

Together they pushed the dresser in front of the door and wedged it tight with the table.

"I'm going to take a shower," said Malko. "You go to bed."

When he came out of the bathroom nothing was visible of her but her hair. He slipped into bed. She deliberately turned her back and said goodnight in a sulky voice. They were almost touching, and Malko could smell her delicious perfume.

He lay awake, the events of the last two days whirling endlessly around in his tired brain.

They had begun when the telephone rang in his house at Poughkeepsie, and the head of the CIA Middle-Eastern sector came on the line.

"Can you meet me for lunch in Washington tomorrow?"

The ritual question. Malko was running short of money. Restoring his castle was costing a fortune, and he had to get the roof of the east tower finished before winter set in.

Thirty thousand. . . . Once the castle had belonged to his family. He had bought it back for a song before the war. The only thing was, every stick and stone needed restoration. So he worked for the CIA.

They liked him in Washington, for two reasons. One was his extraordinary memory: he could talk to someone for five minutes and remember his Christian name thirty years later. And this gift had enabled him to acquire some twenty out-of-the-way languages, like Turkish and Persian.

The other reason was that he had a particular hatred of everything that was Communist, because the Russians had annexed the park belonging to his castle and put it on the wrong side of the Iron Curtain.

But he still had the main building. And that was why Malko arrived punctually the next day in the little restaurant on quiet N Street. William

Mitchell was there already. The meal passed uneventfully; then, when the coffee had been brought, Mitchell said:

"Prince Malko, I'm in the shit."

Malko laughed.

"What misfortune have our Muscovite colleagues inflicted on you this time?"

"Oh, *they* haven't done anything."

"Then it's the Yellow Peril."

"No, worse."

"Well, De Gaulle is dead now, I don't understand."

"Listen. What I'm going to tell you is so secret that it would only be safe if we went to the middle of the New Mexico desert and discussed it there.

"Two days ago the President sent for me. He'd just had a top secret message from Moscow on the hot line. Soviet Intelligence claims that the CIA in Teheran is planning a nice little revolution, in which they will assassinate the Shah and replace him with one of their own men."

"Just like that?"

"Oh, that isn't all. The Russians didn't just pass on the tip. They made it clear that if it wasn't straightened out they'd treat the coup as an act of aggression, and the 1948 treaty would then allow them to invade northern Iran. Furthermore they'd take it that he, the President of the United States, was incapable of controlling his agencies. You can imagine the consequences.

"The President got very, very sore. He gave me fourteen days to find out what's going on, and if necessary do something about it.

"Now that's all fine and dandy, except for one thing. Our top man in Teheran is a fellow called General Schalberg. One helluva tough cookie. When Mossadegh got the bum's rush in '52, Schalberg was the guy who did the rushing. He knows Iran like you know your own backyard and is the

18

best friend of General Khadjar, the head of the Shah's Secret Police."

"Why don't you just recall him?"

"That's not so easy. For one thing, we don't have a valid reason—official reason, that is. If he smells a rat, and the story we've heard is true, we could have an incident on our hands. And . . ."

He did a little mime with his hands, expressive of a somewhat violent incident.

"Suppose it's all a Russian invention?"

"Could be. Schalberg's their public enemy number one. This'd be a pretty cute way of putting him on the spot. You couldn't prove a thing, they'd just pretend he'd been preparing a coup and that we'd stopped him. Only we can't take the risk."

"So what do you want me to do about it?"

"Go to Teheran."

"Where I do what? Ask Schalberg—in the nicest possible way—whether he's planning to assassinate the Shah, and fix me for an encore?"

"No, you have a cover story. The CIA in Teheran is low on secret funds at the moment. As you know, aid to underdeveloped countries doesn't always get there via the bank. . . . It's kind of tricky, sending six hundred thousand dollars by cable."

Malko was surprised. "Six hundred thousand dollars. They're not all so underdeveloped in Teheran."

"Ah, don't talk to me about that. Two years ago a general cost ten thousand bucks a year; now it's double. And we've no idea what he's really worth.

"Clearly it's too risky to send that sort of money by the diplomatic bag, so no one will be surprised if we use a special secure courier."

"And who's to be the lucky recipient of these six hundred thousand iron men?"

"General Schalberg."

"That's nice. That's what I call a visiting card."

"And when you've delivered you can have a week's holiday in Iran . . ."

"But you need cash and arms to start a revolution . . ."

"That's exactly the point. This money already has a specific destination. And it won't be Schalberg who distributes it. We're just going to give him a little bit of a hand."

"A hand, or a push?"

"No jokes, this is a warning. Be very careful. If anything happens to you we'll know the Russians didn't make it all up."

"That's great. And in the event of your friends not killing me for my money, who're you sending to help clear up the mess?"

"No one. That kind of thing comes under Schalberg's department; let's say you'll be better off without his help. You have one contact, a man called Jean Derieux. He works for us on and off, passed us a couple of good tips about the Suez business when he was in Egypt. He does a little bit for everyone. I wouldn't trust him completely, but he knows the country, and there's quite a few ways he can be useful to you."

"I could ask the Russians for help, too. It's really something, isn't it, when they know more about our own agencies than we do."

"You'd better stick to Derieux."

"What do I do when it's all over? Send you Schalberg in a basket?"

"You have *carte blanche*—repeat, *carte blanche*. If the story turns out to be right you'll have to stop him any way you can, no matter what it costs."

"Well, before I draw up my will I'd like some idea of how much I'll be leaving. What's the prize in this little game?"

The conversation turned to the sordid financial details. When he left, Malko took with him the precious black briefcase. He had never seen so much money.

Mitchell saw him off at the airport, and gave him his final instructions.

"I saw the President, he said to tell you good luck. You *have* to succeed. If you can't do it on your own, you're authorized to inform the Shah. Our ambassador will get you an audience. But remember, that's strictly a last resort, it would mean a terrific loss of face for us."

Sent on his way by these encouraging words, Malko had settled down into his first-class seat and gone to sleep. The journey only started to get interesting at Paris, with the appearance of the delectable Hildegarde.

Malko's eyes were open in the gloom. He looked at the form stretched out beside him. A dim light trickled through the curtains. It must be nearly three. The next day was going to be a tough one.

Hildegarde shifted slightly. Her leg touched his, soft and warm. Suddenly Malko wasn't tired any more. But Hildegarde slept with little, delicious sighs.

There was only one thing to do. Noiselessly he got out of bed, took hold of the base of the lamp and eased it toward the edge of the bedside table. In a single movement he gave it a final shove and slipped back into bed.

It fell with an appalling crash.

Hildegarde screamed and sat up with a start. She grabbed Malko and instantly flung herself into his arms.

"What was that?" she murmured, "I heard a noise."

"Don't know; I was asleep."

"I'm scared."

"Don't worry. I expect it was just a bird hitting the window."

He tightened his arms around her. The whole length of her body was pressed against his. Very slowly he began to stroke her back.

21

"Go back to sleep," he murmured.

He continued to caress her. Little by little his hand slid lower. He felt her body tremble, and press against his own.

There was nothing left but to slip the little nightdress off. She said nothing, but locked her arms around him.

The rest was a matter of skin.

At nine o'clock the heat was stifling. Malko had his breakfast next to the swimming pool, surrounded by American businessmen. Hildegarde was still asleep; he had left her room on tiptoe. Now, showered, shaved and wearing an impeccable black alpaca suit—he felt distinctly better.

He went to the reception desk and asked for the telephone. Mitchell had given him all the numbers he would need. There was no answer from Schalberg's; he tried several others, and then the embassy. Eventually a sleepy voice told him that the general was on a trip in the interior, and would be gone three or four days. He had to deliver the money to Schalberg himself.

Another problem was his contact with Washington. There again he could not afford to use the general's office.

He must get that damned briefcase somewhere where it would be secure while he waited. Assuming, that is, that Schalberg really was out of town. The best thing, Malko decided, would be to put it in a bank. He got up, left the swimming pool and went back to the reception desk.

The Iranian clerk told him that the Bank Melli, on Ferdowsi Avenue, had safe-deposit boxes.

"Get me a cab, will you?"

"Certainly, sir."

The clerk came with him to the door, and snapped his fingers. An ancient Mercedes 190D left the line of cabs and pulled up in front of them. The driver, like most Iranians, was unshaven, and his

22

looks did not exactly inspire confidence, but looks weren't everything.

He climbed in, and the taxi shot off toward Teheran.

The traffic in the center of town was indescribable. Aged trucks and overloaded buses duelled with ragged taxis, patched and covered with white-daubed slogans. Veiled women stood at the roadside, waiting for one of the collective taxis to decide to stop.

The American car following Malko's taxi was six years old. He had noticed it as he left the Hilton, on account of the network of cracks covering its windshield. There were two men in it, but they were too far away for him to identify them.

It was reasonable to suppose that their intentions toward him and his briefcase were less than charitable. He began to want to get to the bank very badly, though in the middle of all the traffic he felt curiously safe.

His taxi painfully negotiated the crossing of the Avenue Shah Reza, the great boulevard that bisects Teheran from east to west. The other car followed.

Now he could see the Bank Melli quite clearly. But to get inside he must first cross the pavement, a matter of five yards. He gave the driver his fifty rials, and looked around. The Ford with the broken windshield had pulled up just behind, but the two men did not get out. Malko recognized them now. They were the toughs who had kidnapped him the night before.

A brace of uniformed cops were sunning themselves in front of the entrance to the bank. Malko shouted at them "*Ara!*"

Which is to say "come here" in Persian. They stared at him, but remained motionless; eventually the violence of his gesticulations persuaded them to amble over. In Persian Malko explained that he had a briefcase with him containing something of

23

great value, and that he wanted them to escort him to the bank.

They seemed a bit surprised, but arranged themselves obediently on either side of him. He felt better.

He shot a glance back over his shoulder. The two men had quietly got out of their car and were walking behind him, in a far from threatening manner.

The hall was cool and dark. Malko asked at once for the manager's office. He was shown to a little anteroom, and an ancient attendant brought him a cup of green tea on a small silver tray.

Five minutes later another door opened, and a large, distinguished-looking Iranian beckoned. With a mounting sense of relief Malko jumped up and, clasping the briefcase to him, hurried into the office. And stopped short. The two men sat on two chairs, like two *bona fide* customers.

The director spoke before Malko could open his mouth.

"These gentlemen wished to speak to you," he said in English. "It would appear that you have brought money into Iran illegally."

So that was it.

"What right have they to interfere with my business?" Malko protested indignantly.

"These gentlemen are the 'sovak', the local police."

Light flooded in. Malko took out his diplomatic passport, and showed it to the Director.

"I'm a diplomat; I can't be arrested. If you try to do so you'll find yourselves in serious trouble."

He handed the passport to one of the men; he looked at it for a long time, then handed it back.

"There's no question of your being arrested, Mr. Linge," he said in excellent English. "I simply want to see inside your briefcase. Or is that covered by diplomatic immunity as well?"

Malko cursed silently; he should have thought

of that. With the seal of the diplomatic bag, these apes would have no authority.

"*I* am covered by diplomatic immunity," was all he could say. "I must ask you to call the American embassy at once."

"First open the case," said the man. "Or we'll break it open."

Clearly there was no point in trying to bluff his way out of that one. Malko took out his key, put the case on the director's desk, and opened it. The first heavy took hold of it and turned it upside down. For the second time the wads of bills tumbled out. The director gave a start.

"Have you a permit to bring such an amount of dollars into Iran?" the man asked softly.

It was time for a change of tactics. Malko turned to the director and said sharply: "I insist that you have these men arrested immediately, and call my embassy. They're gangsters; yesterday they attacked the bus I was in to steal this briefcase."

The director looked distinctly worried.

After a short pause he managed to say: "These gentlemen are from the secret police. I have seen their identification cards. I can do nothing to stop them. And in any case your affairs do not seem to be, er, entirely in order."

That was unanswerable.

The heavy calmly put the packets of money back in the case. Malko watched him, hypnotized. To be unloaded of six hundred thousand of the U.S. government's dollars was not a good beginning.

"What are you doing?" he demanded.

"I'm confiscating this money," the man replied equably.

"Then I'm coming with you," said Malko. "This is robbery."

"That's impossible. I have no authority to take you along, you're protected by your diplomatic passport."

"That's very true," interposed the director.

"You can go to police headquarters later today if you want," the man explained.

"Certainly not," Malko snapped. "I'm coming with you right now."

"That's impossible," repeated the man, completely serious, "We have to conduct other investigations."

He gave a sign to he second hoodlum, who had until then remained silent. He now left the room, to return two minutes later with one of the two uniformed policemen. He gave him an order in Persian; the cop went over to the door and fixed Malko with a threatening gaze.

"This officer has instructions not to let you leave for ten minutes," explained the more talkative of the heavies. "He will use any means he thinks fit."

Malko was ready to explode with annoyance and frustration. He watched the precious briefcase disappear, swinging gently in the man's hand. When the men had gone he turned again to the banker.

"You are an accomplice in this theft!" he shouted. "I warn you, my embassy won't leave it at this. And you're the director of a bank! That's just great!"

The director looked very unhappy.

"They threatened me. They really are from the secret police. You've no idea what they can do. Their boss is General Khadjar; the cemeteries are full of his enemies."

Khadjar. That was Schalberg's friend. Together they had overthrown Mossadegh and drowned the pro-communist Toudeh party in rivers of blood. People living near the secret police headquarters were kept awake by the sound of screaming. It was said that when Khadjar himself could not sleep he would go down into the cells and torture a prisoner to death, to settle his nerves. His speciality was Indian clubs; he broke his victim's bones one by one, starting with the fingers and ending with the head.

26

Malko had seen photographs. A giant, always elegant in a white uniform, with a beautiful black mustache.

The director went on, "If you really are a diplomat it'll all sort itself out. They won't be able to do anything to you. Obviously, the money . . ."

"Have you ever seen smugglers depositing six hundred thousand dollars in a bank?" grated Malko. "Even here that couldn't happen."

That seemed crushing enough, so he left. The cop politely disappeared, a disciplined, one-track man; the money was gone.

Malko went for a walk, to calm his seething brain. There were almost no other Europeans around. Several times he was cornered by carpet sellers. A prayer mat was all he needed . . .

The sun got hotter and hotter. Malko looked for a bar. Inevitably, he failed to find one. He saw nothing but filthy cafés that only sold *aba-li* (a disgusting mixture of lemonade and yoghurt) or the local beer.

Suddenly he thought of the expatriate journalist that Mitchell had mentioned. No better time to find out who one's friends were.

He went into a café.

"*Telephone khodjas?* (Where is the telephone?)"

The owner pointed toward the counter.

Malko dialed. A voice answered in Persian:

"*Baleh?* (Yes?)"

"*Harroyé Derieux befar me?* (Is Mr. Derieux in?)"

"That's me."

In French, this time. An almost imperceptible, indefinable accent.

"I'm a friend of Mr. Mitchell, of Washington. I'd like to see you."

"Okay. You know where I am?"

"Uh-huh. I'll take a cab."

He put a five-rial piece on the counter and left.

A taxi cruised past. Malko gave the Belgian's address: 62 Soraya Avenue.

They drove north out of town, along the road to the Hilton. After nearly twenty minutes the taxi turned into a rough side-road, and drew up in front of a villa surrounded by a high wall.

Malko rang the bell, and set off a furious noise of barking. Paws scratched on the gravel, and the muzzle of a very large dog pushed under the door, displaying an alarming row of white fangs.

The door opened, and Malko took an instinctive pace backwards. The dog was on a leash, however, held by a tall blond man with a big straggling mustache and a monstrous cast in one eye. A rather likeable face.

"Don't worry," he said jovially, "he only bites gardeners. He's a very well brought up dog. Here, look."

He took off the animal's collar and said: "Go on, Turk." The dog bounded off toward a gardener, who took off for the house like a rabbit. Derieux roared with laughter.

"The bastard ruined one for me once, y'know. But I've got the best gardeners in Teheran. They know that if they let themselves give in to their natural laziness they'll get eaten."

Malko followed his host into the house. It was somewhat perfunctorily furnished, but there was a big swimming pool.

"Let's have a drop of champagne," suggested Derieux.

He disappeared, and returned a moment later with a case. He set about prying off the lid. An inscription in big black letters on the side said "German embassy, Teheran".

Derieux grinned hugely and explained:

"I buy my champagne from the Iranian customs officers. They have the best. They systematically remove a quarter of every consignment, and bring it straight here."

He filled two glasses.

"Filthy! These diplomats have no idea at all of how to live. Now, what ill wind blows you here? I take it you didn't come to Teheran for a vacation."

Malko hesitated for a moment. He did not feel altogether sure of this fellow. But there was not much choice. He decided to tell him about the briefcase. When he had finished, Derieux shook his head.

"Not much chance of your getting that money back. Especially if they were cops. Khadjar's a real bastard. He sure as hell wouldn't pass up six hundred thousand bucks. They won't have any trouble finding a legal excuse to hang on to it."

"Suppose I asked Schalberg to intervene?"

"And suppose you lit a candle at Lourdes. He and Khadjar are like Siamese twins; they have too many corpses in common. They've run this country for ten years, with the Shah as a figure-head."

"What part does the Shah play in all this?"

"He counts the corpses. Up till now that's suited his book, the Iranian budget doesn't stretch to the cost of keeping political prisoners alive. But I don't think he turns his back when Khadjar comes to call."

"Do you think there'll be a revolution?"

"Well, you know, in the East things aren't as simple as all that. They don't have political parties as such. Every now and then some guy gets it into his head that he'll be the big cheese and starts a fight. He winds up prime minister, or king, or hanged, or shot."

Malko listened, silent and thoughtful. Derieux seemed to know the country pretty well, and he clearly had his head screwed on. Maybe he could be really useful.

"But you didn't come here just to tell me your problems," the journalist went on. "I'm not the lost property office."

"You're quite right," Malko admitted. "The

29

point is I'm on a top secret mission. That's why Washington gave me your name."

"But you have your own guys here."

"Sure. But Washington has the idea that Schalberg's getting a bit too involved in Khadjar's interests, and not enough in ours. I'm here to check that out."

"If you're not careful we'll both be checking out, period."

"I'm a very careful guy. The question is, will you help me?"

"How much?"

"Sixty thousand dollars if you get the briefcase back—full. Otherwise, ten thousand plus expenses. But you'll have to trust me. I can't pay you immediately, for obvious reasons."

Derieux pretended to look thoughtful.

"Okay, that's how we'll leave it. But there isn't much chance of success."

"I know that. But it gives us a good excuse for bringing you in. As Schalberg's out of Teheran today I'll tell him that I called on you while he was unavailable. *D'accord?*"

The Belgian filled his pipe, nodding.

"That'll do, but let's hope they don't go into it too deeply. Let's start by paying Khadjar an official visit. Hang on a minute, I'll just put some clothes on."

Soon Derieux reappeared, and they got into his Mercedes 220. The dog followed the car as far as the main road.

Back into the stifling heat—it couldn't have been less than a hundred and five. At the crossroads the cops sheltered under little canvas awnings, sluggishly directing a terrifying whirl of traffic. The Belgian headed for the southern part of the city, and eventually drew up in a square crowded with watermelon-vendors.

"Here we are. We'll ask to see Khadjar, so get out your diplomatic passport."

The traditional unshaven attendant led them to a waiting room. The heavy pistol tucked into his belt was the only indication that they were in a government building.

"That reminds me," said Malko, "you must get me a gun. They took mine."

"When we get back," Derieux said with an air of lordly beneficence, "you can choose whatever you need."

Clearly a man of great hospitality.

Nearly an hour passed. Malko's temper deteriorated. Finally the attendant returned and showed them into a spacious office, where they were received by a man with enough braid and medals for a field marshal; Malko was very let down when he introduced himself as Major Hosrodar.

Derieux had met him before, and the next five minutes were occupied by their mutual *salaams*. Eventually Malko was allowed to speak. The major listened, unblinking.

"I know nothing about this," he declared, abstractedly leafing through Malko's passport. "I shall have to go and make some inquiries. Will you wait for me here, please."

His English was perfect. He made a nice little bow, and faded.

"A shark," Derieux muttered. "Khadjar's right-hand man. If they were real cops he'll know. And if they weren't he'll be able to find out long before we could, just by making a few phone calls."

"Do you think Khadjar wanted the six hundred thousand for himself?"

"I think he'd appreciate that kind of windfall. Anyway, we'll soon see."

Tea came. Twenty minutes later Major Hosrodar reappeared, looking concerned. He sat down at his desk, and turned to face Malko.

"As you thought, you have had the misfortune to be set upon by a gang of common swindlers. There is no record here of such an operation involving you. I shall put you and your case into the hands of the officer in charge of criminal inquiries."

He rose and spoke swiftly to Derieux in Persian, giving him directions.

They had to pass through a labyrinth of filthy corridors, reeking of urine and sweat. Eventually they found the door they were looking for. The glass panel bore the name of Captain Shid.

Tea, again. Nice little bows, again. Explanations, again. Captain Shid was friendly, smiling. Yes, his superior, Major Hosrodar, had told him all about it. He was awfully sympathetic, but in a big city, you know? He personally would see that effective action was taken. He seemed so determined that Malko's hopes rose again for a moment. Then he outlined his plan.

"According to your statement you know what sort of car these two gangsters used. I'm going to give you two of my uniformed officers. Teheran isn't such a big place. I recommend you stand at the intersection of Shah Reza and Ferdowsi Avenues; the car is bound to pass, and you'll be able to point it out to my men. They'll whistle, it'll stop, and then it'll just be a matter of catching them."

For a full minute Malko said nothing. He examined the officer's face for some sign of amusement, but in vain.

"But aren't you going to have a proper investigation?" he finally protested.

The captain made a gesture intended to be placatory. "Yes, yes, of course, but we have very few leads. If I even knew these men's names . . ."

"You don't think the director of the Bank Melli . . . ?"

"They had forged police passes, so presumably they gave false names."

There seemed to be no possible reply. For an instant Malko had an image of himself wandering round Teheran with a brace of cops tagging along at his heels.

"Well, thanks for all your help," he said, "but I'm afraid I really don't have the time to stand around at street corners. Perhaps you could put the two men there without me."

The officer smiled, but said nothing. The interview was over.

Malko had to get out before he broke something. Back in Derieux's car he exploded.

"Why didn't you say something? That guy made complete fools of us!"

Derieux shrugged his shoulders, and slammed on his brakes to avoid a taxi.

"Waste of time. That's the Iranian way of conning you. They never say no, but pretty soon you think you're going crazy. If the chief of police talked like that in any other country you'd have thrown him out of the window; here you thank him.

"It's damn neat. The director of the bank won't say anything, he'll be too scared of another visit from old man Khadjar's gestapo. Your two friends'll be on a mission to the Pakistani border or somewhere by now, and the police simply bust themselves with goodwill and cooperativeness. . . . But there's one thing that bothers me . . ."

"Which is?"

"Khadjar's information seemed particularly good. I wonder if your friend Schalberg earned his cut of the loot already?"

"I still have a card to play," said Malko thoughtfully. "But it means waiting for him to get back. We'll see Khadjar together."

"What is it?"

"It'll be a nice surprise for you. There's no point in telling you, and it could get you into trouble if you knew."

Derieux shrugged, and let it go.

"Let's go to the Hilton and have a vodka and lime," he shrugged instead. "We can plan our campaign. It's much too hot now; even revolutions need a break."

Malko agreed at once. Hildegarde would be awake by now. She was leaving the next day, and he didn't want to waste the time that remained. The two men arrived at the Hilton just in time for lunch. There was a message in Malko's box.

"General Schalberg will see you at his office tomorrow. A car will collect you at 10.00 hours."

CHAPTER THREE

Hildegarde wasn't alone. She was stretched out on a chaise longue beside the swimming pool, with a man sitting at her feet. Malko could only see his back.

"That yours?" asked Derieux, pointing. "You better get your ass in gear, dolls like that don't grow on trees round here."

Hildegarde saw Malko coming and waved delightedly. Her companion leapt to his feet like a jack-in-the-box. He was lobster-red, and there were little rolls of flesh round the top of his trunks.

"Hello; my name's Van der Staern," he told Malko. "I hope you don't mind my talking to the lady; it gets very boring here at the hotel."

He had no need to introduce himself. His nationality might have been more obvious if he had had a Belgian flag painted on his round stomach.

Hildegarde watched Malko with sparkling eyes, but he saw only her legs. Long, slender, soft-thighed. It really was very pleasant to be able to look forward to them.

"You must all be my guests for lunch," Van der Staern proclaimed. "Right here, by the swimming pool. I'll go and arrange it at once."

Without waiting for a reply, he shot off like an arrow in search of the *maître d'hotel*.

Malko sighed, and went up to change. Derieux had already started to ogle Hildegarde.

The table was set when he came down again. Hildegarde stretched and strolled up and down a little at the water's edge, generating a wave of baffled lust. Malko wondered what excuse he could find to drag her off for a siesta after lunch.

The Belgian had done rather well by them. There were two big jars of the local speciality, Beluga caviar, for a start. Not that there's anything much else that you can eat in Iran.

Malko gazed in fascination at the color of Van der Staern's flesh. He looked as if he had been immersed in boiling water. He must have been in agony, for the skin was coming off his back in great shreds. The Belgian noticed Malko staring and nodded.

"I know," he sighed, "it's not so good. I'm not used to it, you see I come from Antwerp, and when I got here I thought I'd get a bit of a tan to impress my friends in the chambers . . ."

"Chambers?" Malko cut in.

"Yes, I work for Maître Bosch, notaries at Antwerp for three generations. I'm his senior clerk," he added modestly.

"So you grabbed the cash and lit out for the land of the Arabian Nights?" Malko asked cheerfully.

The other leapt up, scandalized. "I have worked, Monsieur, for Maître Bosch for the past ten years. He trusts me completely."

"Precisely," Malko nodded.

"On the contrary," said Van der Staern, ignoring the adverb, "I am engaged in the most important task of my career."

"Here?"

"Yes. Actually," he confided, "it's all terribly unfortunate. You see, Maître Bosch lent a certain sum of money to an Antwerp businessman, a perfectly sound man, to finance a transaction involving a large cargo of wheat. Bought in Argentina, shipped via Antwerp, for resale in Iran. Everything was in order, and Maître Bosch went ahead with the loan." He was almost in tears. "The Iranian

36

commercial attaché had even given the deal his blessing."

"And then?" demanded Derieux, beginning to chuckle as the outrageousness of the swindle dawned on him.

"Then the wheat was put on a train, and crossed the frontier at Khorramshahr. Up till then everything went perfectly. Then our client got a telegram from his correspondent here, saying that at the last minute the Iranian authorities had refused to give an import license, and in any case the buyers didn't have the money."

"Who are the buyers?"

"Oh, various Iranian official organizations."

"And what about the wheat?"

Van der Staern flung his hands in the air, and nearly choked on his caviar.

"The wheat? The wheat's rotting! It's been sitting in the sweltering heat at Khorramshahr docks for eight days. It's sprouting, swelling till it bursts, it's turning green and yellow, it's absolutely disgusting! And there's nothing I can do about it.

"I've tried everything. There's always another signature to get, or the official I have to see can't be found. One of them even wanted a bribe before he'd give the license."

"Did you pay?" Derieux interrupted.

"Certainly not. I reported it to my embassy."

"And do you have the license?"

"Well, as a matter of fact . . ."

Derieux laughed silently. That wheat would still be at Khorramshahr when harvest time came around again.

"But what are you supposed to do about all this?" asked Malko. He had placed his hand on Hildegarde's knee under the table, and his spirits had improved.

"The man who borrowed the money has surrendered his rights to Maître Bosch, and now the wheat belongs to us. My job's to come to the best

37

possible arrangement. But such trouble I've had! This country is quite impossible! I had the buyer's address; I went there expecting to find a proper establishment with a sign outside, employees, bankers' references, etcetera, etcetera ... and what was there?"

He lowered his voice.

"A merchant in the bazaar! Back in Antwerp I wouldn't give him a hundred francs' worth of credit. He hasn't a bank account, he can hardly read and write! And his shop—if you can call it a shop—turned out to be a pitch-dark booth made out of bits of old packing-cases, at the bottom of the worst alley in the bazaar, and he's buying eighty thousand dollars' worth of wheat. I wanted to know what his assets were; so he pulled a bundle of filthy notes with an elastic band round them from under his *djellaba*. *That* was his capital.

"I threatened to attach his property; he said his shop wasn't worth more than three thousand tomans, and in any case, you know, in Iran you just don't attach ...

"I don't dare try to speed things up. I have one last chance. Apparently his usual customers have no money, but there's some fellow who'll take the whole shipment at a reasonable price. I have to go and see him tomorrow."

"Tomorrow," said Derieux scornfully. "*Farda ... passfarda* ... that's the first Persian word you learn. They never say no here. Just *farda*. Comes to the same thing."

Van der Staern seemed undiscouraged, however. Perhaps the vodka had cheered him up. Anyway, lunch finished on a wave of high spirits. Malko's mind was on Hildegarde. She was like a sleek pussycat, crossing and uncrossing her long slender legs and gazing languorously around the table. Van der Staern must have been blushing, but it didn't show; and he was the first to leave. Derieux followed suit soon after.

"I'm going to wander round," he told Malko, "and see what the word is. Meet you tomorrow after you've seen Schalberg. No point in rushing things."

When Malko got back to the pool Hildegarde had already gone upstairs. He hurried, and they reached her door simultaneously. After that things got very much better. She wanted to shower, and so did he. They collapsed, dripping, on the bed.

In the five-star Darband Hotel, opposite the Summer Palace, is the Kolbeh, one of Teheran's most elegant nightspots. Malko and Hildegarde were headed there for dinner. As they crossed the hotel lobby they passed a Scandinavian Airlines crew assembling in a corner, getting ready to leave. There were four blonde stewardesses.

"Margaretha!" said Hildegarde suddenly, and the tallest of the four flung herself into her arms.

"Margaretha's my best friend," Hildegarde explained. "She works for SAS but we shared an apartment in New York."

Malko did his little bow, and invited the Swedish girl to join them for a drink. He was very worried: he had to tell Washington about the stolen money without the message going through the embassy. Obviously an uncoded cable was out of the question. The telephone couldn't be trusted from one side of Teheran to the other. Hildegarde was leaving for Bangkok in the morning. But . . .

"Where've you just come from?" he asked Margaretha.

"Tokyo, in two hops. First Hong Kong and Manila, then two days' rest in Bangkok. Then Calcutta and Karachi, then Teheran."

"And now you're off to Europe?"

She nodded. "Our DC 8 leaves at five past two this morning. We stop off at Rome and Zurich, and get to Copenhagen at ten."

"Christ, that's quick," he said, surprised.

39

Flattered, she said, "Yes, the super DC 8 is the quickest of all the jets. Cruises at six hundred."

Malko thought for a moment. Then he said: "Would you do something for me—something terribly important?"

"If I can."

"Well, would you telephone someone for me when you get to Copenhagen? Or, better still, give the message to a stewardess on a New York flight, and ask her to call a Washington number when she lands."

Margaretha hesitated for a moment. Hildegarde quickly cut in:

"Say yes, it's for a friend, and it's not against the rules."

"Okay, I'll do it," exploring in her handbag. "Hold on, I'll just check the Copenhagen–New York schedule."

She leafed through a pocket timetable. "Yes, look, Sunday there's just the one flight, the daily one. SK 915, takes off from Copenhagen at fifteen forty-five, gets into New York at nineteen fifteen. I'll have time to get hold of one of the girls. What's the message?"

"That's great," said Malko. "I'll take your address in case you can't get it through; I have a friend in Copenhagen who'll call you."

She scribbled her name and address on a scrap of paper. Malko pocketed it, and went off to send a cable to the third secretary at the embassy, who had certain specialized responsibilities. A number after his name indicated that it was that of a CIA "black" agent.

He gave Margaretha a sheet of paper with a few short sentences written on it. Then he and Hildegarde watched the SAS crew collect their baggage and leave. And then they went on to the Kolbeh.

They spent the rest of the evening there. Hildegarde had to get up at six the next morning, so they went back to the hotel quite early. Before he went up to bed, Malko sent a cable: "Urgently contact stewardess Margaretha Johnson arriving flight Royal Viking Tokyo–Copenhagen 10:00 Sunday," followed by the girl's address and number. If the report didn't get there now ...

Hildegarde was waiting for him, in a blue nightdress.

As he fell asleep a low resonance shook the windows. He looked at his watch: 2:10. Exactly on time, the SAS DC 8 and his message flew off to Copenhagen.

General Schalberg was a shaven-skulled giant. His almond-shaped blue eyes held about as much expression as chips of glass. He smoked ceaselessly, long cigarettes in an amber holder.

But his welcome seemed warm enough. A long black Chrysler had collected Malko from his hotel—it was driven by the first clean-shaven Iranian he had seen to date. Schalberg was waiting in his office when he was shown in; he eyed Malko appraisingly. Malko eyed him back.

Malko sank into a deep armchair, the general towering over him. He didn't seem to know it was an old trick. Unaffected by feelings of inferiority, Malko recounted the story so far, and without pausing demanded:

"Why wasn't I met at Mehrabad? We could've saved ourselves six hundred thousand dollars."

The general's mouth tightened.

"The coded cable got stranded on my desk. I was up north visiting some Iranian agents who had infiltrated the Soviet border. Washington should have given me more notice."

"Maybe. But you could have left *after* you got the cable."

"Don't worry about it," the general said. "I'll take full responsibility. It'll all go in my report tonight."

"You don't have any idea how they got wise?"

41

"The cable was on my desk for two days. Naturally, that much money would be a big temptation. But we shouldn't have any difficulty finding out if there's a black sheep in the family. I'll have a word with my old friend General Khadjar, he may be able to help."

That was the word Malko had been waiting for.

"General Khadjar? He's a very interesting man; I wonder, could you arrange for me to meet him?"

Schalberg scarcely faltered in his stride.

"Why, sure. I'm going there right now, why don't you come along."

They stood up: he still towered over Malko by nearly a foot. They took the elevator. The general's offices were in a small three-story ultra-modern building in the embassy courtyard. All the most important departments were grouped round this courtyard; no major decisions could be taken without the general's knowledge.

The Chrysler was waiting for them. Schalberg's affability increased as they glided through the streets.

"Now your mission's over, why don't you stay in Iran for a few days? I can lend you a car and a driver if you want to visit the Caspian or the Persian Gulf."

"Well, thank you, General, I might take you up on that; but I'd like to see Teheran first."

"Oh, there's nothing to see here, it'll take you a couple of hours at the outside. But Isfahan and Shiraz you really can't afford to miss."

They pulled up in front of the now-familiar building. The general was in civilian clothing, but the sentries presented arms just the same.

General Khadjar's office was on the first floor. Four men with submachine-guns stood on alternate sides of the corridor. Beyond that two toughs lounged in an anteroom, their pockets heavy with artillery.

The door was open; Schalberg went in without

knocking. General Khadjar sat at his desk in a spotless white uniform, looking even more impressive than his photographs. His skin was curiously lusterless, his hair and mustache glossy black, and his eyes wandered incessantly to and fro. He treated Malko to a white-fanged smile like a tiger's, while Schalberg made the introductions in English and recounted the tale of the disappearing briefcase. Khadjar nodded.

"I know about this. His Highness Prince Malko has already spoken to us about it. I will be keeping him informed of any future developments."

The general did not seem worried.

But he did seem a little irritated that his colleague had brought Malko along. Malko noticed that one of the drawers near Khadjar's right hand was open. Clearly a man of prudence.

Schalberg looked embarrassed. Malko sensed this, so he decided to come to his rescue.

"General," he said to Khadjar, "I'm sure you'll do everything possible to find these criminals, and I'm very grateful. But would you also do me another favor, nothing at all to do with this business? Several years ago I knew an Iranian officer who was studying in the States, a man called Tabriz. Can you tell me if he's in Teheran?"

"Certainly."

Khadjar pressed a button on his intercom and spoke a few quick words in Persian. Malko listened, and made sure that he was in fact asking about Lieutenant Tabriz.

"Can you wait few minutes?" Khadjar said. "They're calling me back."

The inevitable tea appeared. Boiling hot. Malko waited impatiently for his answer. It was his only chance to put Khadjar on the spot, or at least to throw him off balance.

The intercom buzzed; Khadjar took a pencil and scribbled something on a piece of paper, which he then gave to Malko.

43

"This is Lieutenant Tabriz's address. Any taxi will take you there."

Malko took the paper and watched Khadjar closely as he said: "I'd be glad if you'd come with me when I pay this visit, General."

"Come with you?"

Khadjar's surprise was genuine. He looked at Malko inquiringly.

"I'd feel safer. You see, I'm afraid what I told you wasn't strictly accurate; it was Lieutenant Tabriz who attacked me the other night. I'm sure he'll be able to help you in your inquiries. . . ."

CHAPTER FOUR

Khadjar remained prefectly impassive.

"That's very interesting," he observed softly. "I will have this Lieutenant Tabriz in here tomorrow. You must come too, and we shall find out the truth together."

It was the perfect reply. By tomorrow almost anything could happen. If Khadjar really was involved in a coup he'd have no difficulty in parrying this threat. But why had the general given him Tabriz's address so readily? That was very strange. . . .

Khadjar was talking again. "Your Highness, will you do me the honor of being my guest this evening? It's my daughter's twentieth birthday, and I'm giving a small party. Yes? I'll have my car pick you up at eight."

He rose. The interview was over. Schalberg, who had become silent and pensive, accompanied Malko downstairs.

"Why didn't you tell me that you'd identified one of the men who attacked you?"

"You gave me no time, General. And I thought the information would be of more practical use to General Khadjar. Let's hope he finds Tabriz—and our money."

"Let's hope so."

Schalberg became increasingly thoughtful. Malko wondered how far he had been deceived. Well he'd know soon enough. The general was neither a fool nor a weakling. He had understood the trap set for Khadjar. And Malko's failure to say anything to him about it was indicative of a certain lack of confidence.

Malko went back to the Hilton in the car. A Pan Am crew arrived, but no Hildegarde. He took his key and went up to his room.

He took Tabriz's address from his pocket. It could be false for all he knew. Why not check it?

But not alone. He picked up the telephone and asked for Derieux's number.

The Belgian answered the phone himself.

"Are you free for a little excursion in to town?"

"What sort of excursion?"

"Reconnaissance."

"Yes, but not right now, I have a lunch date with the Minister of the Court. I'll be free around four."

"Swell. Bring me some artillery." Derieux burst out laughing.

"Did you say a reconnaissance or an attack? Okay, I'll see you later."

Malko showered and stretched out on the bed. The phone woke him; Derieux, calling from downstairs. He dressed quickly, cursing the heat.

Derieux was wearing an electric-blue suit with an enormous carnation in the buttonhole. His face was even redder than usual; lunch had clearly been well lubricated.

"Where are we going?"

Malko handed him the piece of paper that Khadjar had given him. He glanced at it.

"It's in the south, near Shokufeh. It's pretty run-down round there. What are we looking for?"

Malko explained the situation briefly.

"I'm pretty sure we'll never see this lieutenant—unless we catch him ourselves. He must know a lot about Khadjar and Schalberg—he didn't see the six hundred thousand bucks in a crystal ball, and only Schalberg was supposed to know."

Derieux rubbed his chin. He didn't seem very reassured.

"I'm not so keen to pick a fight with old man Khadjar. He's dangerous, he's very well informed and he does exactly what he likes. If he figures I'm helping you I can be slung out of the country in about ten minutes. If I'm lucky."

"He won't do that, on account of me. I represent the American government."

"And when you've gone? No, I think I'm going to drop the whole damn business right here. I don't need that much trouble. You're a nice guy, but I've got a wife and a couple of kids. Here, have a souvenir."

He opened the glove box and pulled out a great big pistol wrapped in a rag, which he put in Malko's lap. He cut across the traffic and pulled up at the curb.

"You're on Shah Reza," he said to Malko, "any taxi'll take you to the southern part of town. Don't pay more than fifty rials, sixty if he kicks up a fuss."

Malko had not moved. Only his special powers of persuasion could help him now. He turned slowly toward Derieux and stared intently into his face, fixing him with his golden eyes.

"What would you say if I told you that I'm here on a top secret mission, on the orders of the President of the United States himself? Suppose I said the stealing of the 600,000 was strictly a minor misfortune? Listen, I need your help; so I'll be responsible for your safety."

Derieux was unconvinced. He shook his head.

"You won't be able to stop Khadjar getting at me when you're five thousand miles away."

"When I go away there won't be any more Khadjar."

"What?"

Derieux looked surprised. He glared at Malko.

"You want to rub out Khadjar? Why? He's always been useful to you. He's the CIA's right arm

47

here. He's been criticized for it often enough, Christ knows."

"Let's just say that the arm has become more like a tentacle. I can't tell you any more for the moment. Look, if it'll help to prove that this isn't a gag, tomorrow I'll give you an American passport in your own name; a diplomatic passport."

"Phoney?"

"Real. Provided by the U.S. ambassador in Teheran."

Derieux's determination was shaken, but he was still not persuaded. Finally, Malko took an envelope out of his wallet, opened it, and produced a document.

"Read this."

It carried the White House head; the text was very short.

"All representatives of the American administration and armed forces are hereby required to give every possible assistance to the bearer, Prince Malko Linge, in the performance of a mission, affecting the security of the United States, which he is conducting in the Middle East. This order is valid for one month."

It was signed by the President. Malko's life insurance.

"I have the authority to requisition the admiral of the Sixth Fleet," said Malko. "*And* the ambassador. This piece of paper makes me as powerful as the President for a month."

"You're a prince?"

"Yes. I belong to one of the oldest families in Austria."

That was enough for Derieux; he raised no more objections. An *Altesse* impressed him much more than the President of the U.S.A. He shifted gears, and shrugged his shoulders.

"Right, let's go. But I hope you don't screw it up. I like my skin the way it is."

Malko did not answer. It had been a close thing.

48

While Derieux applied himself to the harrying of pedestrians and other road-users, he checked the gun and slipped it into his waistband. It took them twenty minutes to get to the address he had been given.

It was in a little beaten-earth road with open sewers, like hundreds of others in Teheran. They had to leave the car and walk the last hundred yards. The house numbers were in random order. Number 27 was next to number 6. And no one around to ask. They knocked on several doors, but no one came.

Finally Derieux, searching in a corridor, found a visiting card with a name in Persian.

"It's on the first floor," he told Malko. "Funny how empty this dump is."

The card was new, and held in place by a pin. Malko's nerves were on edge. They followed the corridor and found a rickety wooden staircase.

There was one door on the landing. It was slightly open. Stuck to the wood was the same visiting card as downstairs.

Derieux pulled a huge Luger from his belt and cocked it. Malko knocked gently on the door, twice.

No reply. He knocked again.

No sound except their breathing.

"Do we go in?" asked Derieux.

"No."

"Why not? He must have skipped."

"I don't think so. It's a trap. Look." He pointed at the hinges. They were glistening with fresh oil.

"Someone's counting on us finding this room and going in. I should say that someone isn't Tabriz."

"You think there's someone waiting for us in there?"

"Some*thing*. Something rather nasty."

"I have an idea," Malko said.

A heavy wooden ladder stood in a corner of the

49

landing. Malko brought it to the door. There was a hook on the wall opposite. After a moment's hunting he found a piece of string in the corridor; he looped it around the hook, and leaning the ladder against Tabriz's door, tied the other end of the string to it. The ladder was now held by the string so that it was balanced against the door.

"Now," said Malko, "that contraption's going in on our behalf. Got a lighter?"

Derieux handed him his Zippo.

"Now. I set fire to the string. We can get downstairs in the time it takes to burn through. When the string breaks the ladder will push the door open and all we have to do is come back upstairs and inspect the results."

The string started to eat into the hemp. They raced down the stairs and along the corridor.

They were still running when the explosion shook the whole street. Instinctively they flung themselves on the ground. When they got up there were people running all around them. Malko and Derieux slowly returned to the house.

Or what was left of it, which was a heap of smoking rubble.

"Must have been ten pounds of T.N.T.," said Malko with a professional air. "Set off by the door opening.

"We'd have made a cute funeral. With the story of the treason of Lieutenant Tabriz, who preferred death to dishonor."

"You think Khadjar did this?"

"Sure of it. It's going to be quite funny this evening, they probably won't even set a place for me."

"What? You're going to dinner with him?"

"I sure am. At least it'll spoil his evening. I'm supposed to be a ghost by now."

"It was pretty well set up. They'd have collected us with a teaspoon. Much more reliable than having the hired help rub us out. That's why there

50

wasn't anyone around in the street; they must have evacuated it."

They got back to the Mercedes without any further incident. Derieux wove his way skilfully through the traffic jams. Night fell, and a curious violet light illuminated the mountains behind Teheran. Malko just had time to change and shower. He had a lunch date with Derieux the next day, and meanwhile he had a couple of things to attend to. . . .

General Khadjar, resplendent in a white uniform, greeted his guests on the steps of his home near the Franco-Iranian Club. He gave not the slightest sign of surprise when he saw Malko. Either his self-control was exemplary, or his information service was very efficient.

"Come, Prince, I'll introduce you to my daughter," he said.

He took Malko's arm and led him to a buffet set up in the garden.

"This is Saadi. She is twenty today."

Malko bowed. She was twenty, and she was really spectacular. Long, slender legs, a narrow ribcage with firm breasts, a small, hard face, triangular like a cat's, an air of intelligence. An appropriate daughter for such a father. Her green eyes returned Malko's golden gaze.

"My father has told me much about you. I am very pleased to meet you."

Her eyes never left his. The voice was low, assured.

"What do you think of our country?" she went on. "I would be glad to help you discover it, if your work permits the time. . . ."

From such a creature, that could only be an invitation—or a trap.

Malko preferred for the moment to think that it was his hypnotic charm at work again.

51

The rooms were filled with Iranian officers with faces like bandits. They all wore pistols, which went badly with the party dresses. Saadi gazed around. She had a way of looking at men that made even Malko blush.

"I'm giving a party next week," she told Malko. "I'd like you to come."

One could scarcely refuse. Especially as the place was teeming with pretty girls.

"Dance?" suggested Malko.

Saadi's dancing technique was pure sex. Malko told himself that the general must have had an ulterior motive in wishing her on him, but that was no reason not to let her press lithely against him. He would have given a lot to see her face. He gently stroked the hand that he was holding, and her slim fingers responded to the pressure.

Their flirtation was interrupted by Khadjar himself. A glass of champagne in his hand, he called cheerfully to Malko, and forced him to abandon Saadi.

The general slipped his arm in a friendly, protective fashion around his shoulders.

"I shall have some news for you tomorrow," he said. "My inquiries have gone very well today. Perhaps we'll even get your money back."

Malko emptied his glass. The general's supplier was better than Derieux's. But the general had a nerve, considering that the inquiries had all but finished permanently as far as Malko was concerned.

"My car will come for you tomorrow at nine," Khadjar said, then moved away.

A little later, Malko left, after having pressed Saadi's hand rather longer than was necessary.

At midnight he was sleeping the sleep of the just, his pistol under his pillow and the dresser pushed up against the door. Khadjar's people would not be able to do much, unless they blew up the hotel.

Khadjar's car arrived exactly on the hour. It

bore no distinctive markings, but the doorman saluted Malko with a new respect.

The journey took ten minutes. The cops at the corner gave them priority all the way, which made a nice change. The rear seats smelled faintly of good *eau de cologne*. The general was a man of refined tastes.

He was waiting in front of the police headquarters; he gave Malko no time to get out of the car. He wore an air of mystery, and said, "I've good news for you."

The blue Chrysler took off again, Khadjar lit a small Dutch cigar and Malko became very thoughtful. They went right through the southern part of the city and into the suburbs, which consisted largely of open-topped brick-works. Eventually the car stopped at the door of a modern building.

There were three army officers standing in front of it. They saluted Khadjar in an ugly, Germanic fashion, and ignored Malko altogether. Then everyone went down a long corridor, icy despite the heat outside. They passed an infirmary. At the end, Khadjar stood aside to let Malko through first. There was no one in the room, no furniture but a table on which lay a draped form. The walls were grey-green, the windows were closed. An officer quickly stepped forward and removed the cloth.

"Do you recognize that man?" Khadjar asked.

Malko went over. The dead man wore an Iranian army uniform. There was an unpleasant wound in his temple. His face was calm.

It was Lieutenant Tabriz.

"That's the officer who was in command when I was attacked," said Malko. "What happened?"

Khadjar pulled the cloth back again, with the careful gesture of an anxious collector protecting a work of art, and led Malko out of the room.

"He committed suicide. I ordered him to be brought in, but my men arrived too late."

"That was at his home?"

53

"At the barracks. He booby-trapped his apartment, and it blew up yesterday afternoon. It'll be difficult to find his accomplices, as he had no time to talk. He must have needed money to cover a gambling debt. Iranians are terrible gamblers, you know. Still, I'll try to find out who they are. Sir, I must beg you to accept the apologies of the Iranian army."

Malko bowed. It was perfect. If he had opened the door the day before, they would simply have regretted that he had involved himself in the investigations. Poor Tabriz's suicide was—questionable. He was much less dangerous dead than alive.

They drove back in silence. Khadjar got out at his office, and let Malko take the car on to the Hilton, where he was meeting Derieux for lunch.

The Belgian appeared punctually, still in his electric blue suit.

"We're eating Iranian today," he volunteered. "It'll make a change."

They drove downtown. He stopped the car near the Officers' Club, and suggested they walk a little.

"It's near the bazaar," he said. "But I'd rather leave the heap here, otherwise they'll strip it bare. Round here even police cars don't leave their windshield wipers lying around."

The streets were choked with people, and Malko could scarcely keep up with the Belgian. The pavement swarmed with peddlers and children. Every other shop had in its window the acetylene lamps that seemed to form the basis of the Iranian economy.

The restaurant was in the corner of a square which also contained the principal entrance to the bazaar. The windows were filthy, and most of the panes replaced by sheets of cardboard, but Derieux went straight in.

The din was deafening. Every table was crowded with traders from the bazaar, talking and laughing

54

at the top of their voices. The dirt was indescribable, and an acrid smell hung in the air.

A fat man came forward to greet Derieux and show him to a free table, which he wiped with a sweep of his arm. Derieux sat down and said by way of warning:

"Here you eat shashlik and rice. Do you want beer or *aba-li?*"

Malko had no idea what *aba-li* was, but instinct told him to have the beer. Derieux called a waiter and gave their order. At once there appeared a plate of radishes and scented white cheese, and flat loaves of an unfamiliar bread.

"So," demanded Dereiux, "did you see Tabriz?"

"Yes, you might say I did."

He brought the journalist up to date. Derieux, crunching radishes, nodded.

"That's very strange. The Iranians aren't bloodthirsty people. It doesn't make any sense, that they should rub that poor guy out and try to finish us off as well, all on account of a little bread. All they had to do was send him away on some phoney mission for a few weeks."

Malko sniffed cautiously at the plate that had appeared in front of him. The rice was saffron yellow and the meat was cut in long slices and looked like strips of cardboard. Could this be the national dish? . . . He tasted the rice and gagged on the burning hot spices. He took a gulp of flat beer and went on: "There's one other thing, which is connected with why I'm here. What do you reckon about the present political climate; I mean, is the Shah firmly established on his throne?"

Derieux roared with laughter.

"I've been here three years. Every month they tell me there's going to be a revolution. Well, you know it all. . . . Sure, we've been hearing for some time that Khadjar fancies the idea of sitting on that throne. He has plenty of people on his side, and part of the army . . . But first of all you have to ease the Shah off. And that's another matter . . ."

The Belgian cut his meat into tiny pieces and dipped them in a green sauce that the waiter had brought. In an instant his plate was clean. Malko stuck to his rice. The meat was as hard as wood, and smelled like it had been cooked with gasoline.

"So what about the Shah?" he said.

"The Shah's pretty thick-skinned. Someone emptied a gun at him point blank, once, and since then he's been kind of suspicious-minded. When you're with him it's a good idea not to make any sudden movements. He wouldn't mind all that much if his heavies got a bit over-enthusiastic and rubbed you out on the spot."

"And what about Khadjar? Does he trust him?"

"Do you trust a snake? They say the Shah never invites him on hunting parties, in case of 'accidents.' Wait a minute, though; do you think Khadjar wants to assassinate the Shah?"

Malko was only half listening, fascinated by the other man's appetite.

"What? Oh, I can't rule out the possibility."

Derieux bit an enormous chunk off his bread and shook his head in vehement dissent.

"Absolutely impossible," he said with his mouth full. "Your buddy Schalberg would be in on it. Khadjar wouldn't lift a finger without telling him. And they'd need arms for it, anyway, and right now they don't have any."

"How do you know? Do you run guns as well?"

"I've been known to."

"You work for anyone who comes along?"

"No, only the ones who pay," said Derieux, unsmiling. "And I have only friends."

He lit a cigarette contentedly. Suddenly he frowned.

"Christ, I'm beginning to get it. Is Schalberg trying to doublecross you?"

Malko did his surprised bit.

"Doublecross me?"

"Well, his bosses. Helping Khadjar behind your back. If Khadjar took power he'd be able to squeeze the left wing pretty hard . . ."

"Do you think money's the only thing Schalberg's interested in?"

"No, there is one other possible reason: since the beginning of this year the Shah's been on much better terms with the Russians. He's starting to think about neutralism. It'd suit Schalberg to have someone running the country who thinks the same way he does."

Malko sampled a radish. It was the only edible thing in the restaurant.

"Then will you work with me?"

"Now I've come so far, why not? I hope you'll be suitably grateful. And if it goes well the Shah will love me. *He* has some pretty nice ways of showing his gratitude."

A good reason.

Derieux insisted on paying the bill. They crossed the street and looked around.

"Do you think we're being followed?"

"Of course," said Derieux. "It's no problem for them. But they won't try anything serious."

"All the same," said Malko, "I'm going to take one or two precautions. I have to find a lead, and especially I have to find out if there's anything cooking; I'd be happier without a tail."

"I have some sources of information. I can have a try. I'll take you back to the hotel, and we can talk tomorrow."

The traffic was heavy, the Iranian drivers still playing chicken. Malko breathed a sigh of relief when he got back to the Hilton lounge. The heat was suffocating and he had nothing to do. He decided to get his swimming trunks and go to the pool. Perhaps Pan Am had brought a new load of lovelies.

There were no stewardesses beside the swimming

57

pool, but as Malko arrived a familiar figure leaped from its deck chair and flung itself upon him.

It was Van der Staern, an even richer scarlet than before.

"Am I glad to see you! I called your room several times, but there wasn't any answer."

"Are you working up to a proposal?" he asked, deadpan.

Van der Staern bridled.

"Do you spend the *whole* time making jokes? I have something *very* important to ask you," he said coldly.

"Really?"

"But not here."

"Can't it wait till sunset? I really don't want any more exercise today."

"No, you must come at once."

The Belgian was on his feet, hovering insistently. Malko realized that nothing short of drowning him would get Van der Staern off his back.

"Where do you want me to go?"

"To my room."

"Now you listen to me . . ."

"Hush, someone will hear you!"

Van der Staern's nerves were bad. He peered around to see if anyone had overheard Malko. But there was only a waiter, stupefied by the sun, standing fast asleep in a shady corner.

"Okay," said Malko wearily, "let's go."

Van der Staern led the way. His room was on the eighth floor; it was identical to Malko's. They sat in armchairs and looked at each other. The Belgian seemed extremely embarrassed.

"You see," he started, "I feel you know this country much better than me. You understand what one can and can't do, you know?"

He leaned toward Malko.

"The rest of us, you know, we're so used to legality that we don't know. . . ."

58

"In other words," interrupted Malko, "you think I'm a crook."

"No, no, of course not. But you've done business in this country. You have contacts."

Malko had had enough beating about the bush. The honest Mr. Van der Staern must have been cooking up a deal somewhat less than honest.

"Okay, fine, so what do you want me to do?"

Van der Staern rubbed his damp hands nervously together.

"You remember I was telling you about my problems. This morning I went to see my customer. And he had a nice surprise for me. He offered to pay me and he even gave me something on account."

"What more could you ask for?"

"You'll see in a minute. He's going to pay what he owes me, but there's a hitch. The payment isn't exactly, er, legal, if you see what I mean."

"No, I don't," said Malko jokingly.

"He's giving me foreign currency. But I have to get it out of the country without anyone knowing about it. Otherwise I could go to jail, apparently."

This was all very mysterious. Van der Staern was getting his payment in Afghan rials or Siamese tickals; back in Europe he would resell them at ten cents a pound weight.

"What currency is it?" Malko asked, to get the conversation going again.

"Dollars."

Suddenly Malko was listening. People don't get rid of their dollars illegally. It must be Monopoly money. The Belgian mistook his change of expression.

"Are you interested?" he said eagerly. "Can you exchange them for rials for me? I'd never have the nerve to go through the customs with those bills on me. We can come to an arrangement."

Honesty must diminish with latitude.

"Maybe I'd better see them." Van der Staern

suggested. "I'm afraid they might be forged as well."

"Okay."

Van der Staern took a case out from under the bed, and extracted from it a bundle of newspapers. They were wrapped round a packet of hundred-dollar bills.

Malko leaned forward and took the packet from him. He shut his eyes for a moment, and numbers whirled round in his head. His memory was useful at times like this.

He inspected the top bill of the wad with care, and rubbed it gently. It was not a fake. The Belgian stared anxiously.

"This does interest me," Malko said.

The packet of bills was unquestionably part of the stolen six hundred thousand. Malko recognized the numbers, implanted indelibly in his memory.

CHAPTER FIVE

Malko stared at the wads of notes littered on the bed, and his irritation drained away. He hadn't really expected to see any of the money again, and certainly not so soon. Of course it didn't belong to him any more, which was unfortunate. He could hardly turn to Van der Staern and say with a polite smile, "Give me back my money."

One thing still bothered him, too. He said to the Belgian, "These notes seem perfectly okay. But tell me something: how come you're getting a good price for a load of wheat that you said was half rotten and virtually valueless?"

Van der Staern smiled smugly.

"Iranians must be a lot easier to please than Belgians, I guess. I imagine they'll still be able to make nice cakes with that stuff, and at the prices they sell them they won't lose any money. In any case, that's none of my business, nor yours. You haven't answered my question: can you help me out with the currency problem or not?"

"Certainly I can," Malko said coolly, "but before I do I'd like to clear up a couple of points, for my own satisfaction—like where these notes come from, for example. And I want to meet the man who gave them to you, this trader in the bazaar." He saw Van der Staern looking doubtful. "You can introduce me as a possible prospective customer, if you think he'll get suspicious."

"You? A customer? A European?"

"Why not? I'm, let's say, manager of a public-works camp; I have people to feed, haven't I?"

Van der Staern hesitated. The idea didn't seem to appeal much; but he wanted to shift all those dollar bills more.

"All right," he finally said. "We'll go there now. I'll just leave this cash in the safe and meet you downstairs."

Malko went to his room, and took the opportunity of changing his suit, which was getting crumpled. He tried to ring Derieux, but the line was busy.

They drove down in Van der Staern's rented Mercedes. No one followed them. It took them three quarters of an hour to get to the main gate of the bazaar. Inside, the crowds made the ones outside look like a bunch of claustrophobes; a solid mass of heaving, pushing, sweating, shouting people.

The bazaar. An immense tangled maze of covered alleys, thousands of shops, raucous with the din of traders shouting their wares. Some of the people in it did not see daylight for months on end, even sleeping there on the beaten-earth floor. But this was the true economic center of Teheran. Here there was no trust in banks; the merchants lent at twenty per cent per month, lived in rags, but held enormous quantities of liquid cash, concealed in woollen belts under their robes.

Suddenly Malko and Van der Staern caught their breath as they were all but choked by an unfamiliar, acrid smell. They had arrived in the street of the cereal traders. Everywhere sacks of semolina, wheat, soya and maize, reeking with a sickly-sweet, intoxicating stench.

"There it is," said Van der Staern.

It wasn't a lot to look at. No more than ten feet wide, with a wooden shutter. In the front of the shop several sacks of grain stood gaping open, to attract customers. They weren't attracting many. An aged weathered Persian sat in the shadows at the back of the shop. When he saw the Belgian he quickly got to his feet. They went into the shop. Several shaven-headed urchins stared curiously at them.

"Mr. Oveida, may I introduce my friend Mr. Linge?"

The old man bowed and mumbled.

"Mr. Linge," Van der Staern went on, "is interested in the rest of my wheat. As you're having so much difficulty in getting rid of it, he might be able to help us out."

The old man's eyes were half closed, and he seemed to be asleep.

A little boy appeared with three cups of green tea on a tray, and business waited on the rituals of oriental courtesy.

The old man waved his arms about and said in shaky English, "I think there would be no use. My customer has now decided to buy all. If Mr.—er—Linge needs some large amounts of wheat I can find it for him. I expect some semolina from Azerbaijan this week. Not expensive, you pay in rials. A hundred tomans per ton. I show you."

He got up briskly and scooped up some semolina with a bowl from one of the sacks, and tipped it into a little bag.

"You taste, sir."

Even accompanied by tea raw semolina is not really very digestible. Malko politely declined, and returned to his theme.

"The wheat will suit me very well; I'm prepared to pay a good price. More than your other customer."

The old man looked very worried. "Is impossible. I have made commitment. He is very important man. He will not be pleased.

"Anyway," he added, turning to Van der Staern, "you get the rest of your money tomorrow."

"I see," Malko went on relentlessly. "But if I buy the wheat and resell it to your customer, everyone will get something out of it. And since

63

you'll get your commission twice ..." He left the implication open.

But something even more persuasive than that argument was making the old man's mind up for him, and he wouldn't play.

"The wheat is not good," he moaned. "I find you some better. It has been a long time in the sun."

"Then why's your other customer so anxious to get it?"

But the old man's answer was unintelligible; he was shifting about as if the box he sat on was red-hot. He shook with fear, and his beard trembled. But who could be so interested in half-rotten wheat that he would pay for it in precious stolen dollars? And above all, what was there about this particular load of wheat that so interested Khadjar? After all, people with full bellies make poor revolutionaries.

"Too bad," he said, getting up. "Maybe we can do business some other time."

Immediately the old merchant became talkative again, promising Malko a golden future if he would only transfer his interest to the semolina. He came with them to the door, full of apologies and compliments. As they left they nearly collided with two men coming into the shop—two Europeans.

Malko suddenly became very interested in a mound of raisins at the next shop. The two men were speaking in fluent Persian, the old man answering them in a thin, plaintive tone of voice. Malko could not pick up the whole of the conversation, but he gathered that it was about wheat.

The old man was protesting that he had none, though if they wanted some semolina.... That rotten wheat was certainly exciting a good deal of interest. After a round of courtesies the two men left the shop, fortunately turning away from Malko. He fell into step behind them. Van der Staern had stayed a little way away, and was hemmed in by the crowd. He hurried to catch up with Malko.

"What's going on?"

"I don't know. Another customer for your wheat. People are having a hard time keeping away from it. Do you know them?"

"No."

"Good. We'll follow them. This is getting interesting."

It couldn't have been easier. The men were walking quickly without looking around. The crowd was so dense that Malko could safely have gotten even closer.

Eventually they reached the edge of the bazaar, and the men got into a little black car. The Mercedes was parked just behind. Malko drove. The black car headed north on Hafez Avenue. The driver wasn't taking any precautions against being followed. His indicator winked, and he turned into a small side-street and stopped in front of an imposing gateway. He steered up on to the pavement and honked. The gate opened and he drove in. Malko, who had stopped a little way back, started again, and drove slowly past. There was a big brass plate on one of the square gate-pillars; it read 'Embassy of the Union of Sovient Socialist Republics.'

"Well, how about that?"

Van der Staern's eyes widened. Malko looked at him quizzically. "Even the Russians want your wheat. Maybe it's a special variety, with giant ears ..."

The Belgian shook his head. "I don't understand. It's all very strange. But what I do know is that I'm finally going to get paid. Are you still interested in the dollars? I can let you have them at five per cent below."

"More than ever. But there's something that interests me even more than that: your wheat. I'll make a deal with you. I'll take all your dollars, in exchange for whatever currency you like. But you'll come with me to Khorramshahr, so I can have a look at the golden grain."

"To Khorramshahr? You're mad! What on earth for? And what good will it do you to see a lot of sacks of moldy wheat?"

"That's my problem. You can take it or leave it, that's the deal. The wheat and the dollars, or nothing. Take your time, you've got till we get to the hotel to make up your mind."

He flung himself into the delights of the Teheran traffic situation. Van der Staern sat in silence until they were safely back at the Hilton.

"Okay, you win; I'll come with you to Khorramshahr," he sighed. "But I'd like to feel sure that my dollars'll be okay."

"You have my word. Now let's go to the bar and have a drink."

The bar was charming, decorated in the Arabic manner with a little fountain.

They ordered two vodka and limes. Malko drank his in a gulp, and gazed around. The bar was empty except for three Persian girls chattering and drinking green tea. Malko's eye was immediately caught by one of them; she had huge dark eyes and her dress kept few secrets. He stared, fascinated. She sensed that she was being looked at, and sat more upright, her breasts pressing against the silk. Malko ordered another vodka. Amazing. . . . He was wondering how he could start a conversation when she got up and swayed past him. Her legs were long and very slim. Like an automaton Malko got up and followed her. She went straight to the john. Foiled, he waited in the lobby, pacing to and fro. He wanted her very badly. It wouldn't be easy, though. Iranian girls remain virgins until they marry. Afterwards, of course, is another matter . . . but this girl had no wedding ring.

She reappeared at that moment and went over to the newspaper stand in the corner of the lobby. Malko strolled slowly once around the lobby (the

Hilton has a very big lobby) and came up behind her to look over her shoulder. She was reading *Der Stern*.

He said softly, "Do you speak German?"

She turned around. He was glad he had got closer; her lips were full and moist-red, a little parted. He felt his self-control begin to slip.

"Yes, a little . . ." The voice was low and steady. "Are you German?"

"Austrian. Prince Malko Linge; at your service . . ." He bowed very low, with the most agreeable consequences. "I'm a stranger here, and a little bit lost . . . I wonder—might I offer you some tea?"

She hesitated.

"I'd love to, but, you know, I'm not alone. Another time, perhaps."

She put the magazine down.

"Nor am I at the moment. But perhaps we could have dinner some time?"

She stared at him in surprise and amazement. "I'm so sorry, but that is completely impossible. We have not been properly introduced."

"Oh, I see. Then perhaps we could meet during the day—tomorrow, perhaps?"

"During the day I have a job."

"Well, we could meet after you have finished working, in the afternoon. You won't put me off so easily, you know; I find you much too attractive."

She smiled. "All right, phone me tomorrow, then, at my office. The number is 34–527. Ask for Tania Taldeh. I'll try and see you for a moment after work."

Malko gazed longingly at her departing figure.

When he returned to Van der Staern, the Belgian was looking even more depressed than before.

"What the hell are you up to?" he demanded.

Malko tried to look mysterious. "I'm working for your American currency."

Van der Staern grinned broadly; then suddenly

became angry again. "I know what you're doing; you're fooling around with that little girl."

"That's true. But I'm thinking about the dollars as well."

Just then the three girls got up and walked out. They passed right in front of Malko. Tania did not look his way, which annoyed him. He made himself a promise that she would pay for that.

"We'll leave first thing tomorrow morning," he told Van der Staern. "That'll give these friends of mine time to make arrangements for the money, so it'll be all tied up by the time we get back. Right now I've got a couple of things to do, but I'll be back this evening. I'll have a friend with me, by the way; he'll be coming with us. He'll be very useful, he knows the country."

He signed the check and left.

He took the first taxi in the line.

"The bazaar."

If he could get to talk to that merchant on his own, the old man just might have something enlightening to say on the topic of wheat.

Malko pushed unhurriedly through the narrow covered alleys. But once he was immersed in that crowd, he was sorry he hadn't brought Derieux along. A man could disappear here without sound or trace, engulfed by the gigantic milling throng.

He hoped he looked like a tourist out for a stroll. As he came into the street of the grain-merchants he saw out of the corner of his eye that a light was still burning in the old man's shop.

He stood in front of a copper-beater's window and waited. Eventually the old man started to close up; he pulled down his wooden shutters, put out the lamp, hooked an enormous padlock into the rings on the door and jamb, and set off at a brisk pace in the opposite direction from where Malko was standing.

He was easy to follow, but Malko kept his distance. They plunged into the labyrinth, turning abruptly and without apparent pattern to right and left, then suddenly emerged in the south, in a part of the town where the streets were paved with beaten earth and lit by widely-spaced gas lamps.

Still the old man hurried along. Two figures brushed past Malko, walking quickly. Two men, each carrying what looked like a very long, slender bottle. They came level with the old man, one on each side. Before Malko could do anything, one of them thrust the unfortunate merchant roughly against the wall, and the other lifted the thing in his hand and brought it down on the old man's head.

There was an obscene crack of breaking bone, and the old man gave a muffled cry and put both hands up to his head. The first man let him go and hit him in the face, like a lumberjack chopping into a tree. The old man slid down the wall to the ground.

Malko started to run, tugging Derieux's Colt from his belt.

They heard Malko coming, and looked up. One of them returned at once to his efforts, the other turned toward Malko, swinging his club easily by his side. His head was shaven, the face round and fat, with little, angry, restless eyes. Ten feet from Malko he whipped his club up and down again to crush him against the wall. Malko stepped to one side, and a cloud of dust spurted from the wall about where his head would have been.

Already the man was whirling around for a second attempt, while the second murderer had finished battering the old man and now ran to his friend's assistance. No one had spoken.

Malko swung the Colt as hard as he could, and the heavy pistol struck the man on his right temple. He groaned and staggered back; a trickle of blood ran down his face. A normal man would have been finished; he shook his head a little and rushed at Malko again.

69

Malko fired twice, and both men stopped, feeling the wind of the bullets on their faces. The barrel of the pistol was a black tunnel, and they were looking down it.

"Drop it," said Malko in Persian.

They looked surprised, but didn't move. The shots had sounded loud, but the streets were still empty.

"Drop it now, or I'll kill you."

The two men looked at each other, and took a step forward. Malko slowly lifted the barrel of the Colt, and, as one man, they turned on their heels and fled.

He raced after them, but after fifty yards they started to draw away. They turned into a narrow, dark passage, and Malko decided that following them any further would be a mistake.

He walked slowly back. The old man was a pile of rags at the foot of a stone wall. Malko bent over it, feeling sick. His hand touched the head, and his fingers dipped into a mush of hair and splinters of bone. Thank God for the dark.

Just the same he searched the body. Under the robe he found a belt, and pulled it out. It contained papers, and some money. He thrust everything into his pocket, and left in a hurry.

He hadn't the faintest idea where he was, and he must have walked for nearly a quarter of an hour in the deserted alleys before he found a properly lit street. Eventually a taxi stopped. He rode it to the crossing of Shah Reza and Ferdowsi, and from there took another cab to the Hilton.

Poor old bastard. He must have been near to closing the best deal he'd ever made. Malko shivered, and wondered why they hadn't put the finger on himself after his visit to the shop that afternoon. He must have been seen, and whoever was behind it all would have known that the old man would crack under serious questioning. Presumably they'd preferred not to take any chances. Just like Tabriz.

But what was the link between a ragged old bazaar trader and General Khadjar? And why did someone want that wheat so badly that even the Russians were interested?

Back in his room, Malko spread the dead man's possessions out on the bed. There were several dirty invoices and notes, written in Persian, and with a little puzzling Malko managed to decipher them. Apparently the old man wasn't above a little money lending.

Apart from that there was a small amount of money, a creased photograph of a bearded Iman, (a Moslem priest) several other papers of no importance, and an almost clean sheet of white writing paper, folded in quarters.

He smoothed it out flat with unnecessary care. It was covered with European numerals and letters, and scribbled notes in Persian. The digits from one to ten were written in a column, with alongside each one a combination of numbers and letters. Malko copied the first line on to a sheet of hotel notepaper; perhaps it would start to make sense.

1 — 12 M.G. 42. 6. B.Z. 20,000 CA. 30.

It didn't make sense. The other lines were much the same, with variations in both figures and letters. Presumably a code. The Persian writing told him nothing: there were some transliterations of the European numbers and letters, and a lot of words he didn't understand.

He put the money and the coded sheet in his pocket; the other papers he tore up and flushed down the toilet. Then he quickly showered, dressed, and went down for dinner. In the lobby he asked for Derieux's number. He didn't think the telephone in his room was tapped, but this was more secure.

Derieux answered at once. "So what happened to you? I was getting worried."

71

"I was a little nervous myself. Listen, how do you feel about a little trip to the deep south?"

"To where?"

"Khorramshahr."

A pregnant pause. "You are out of your mind," the Belgian carefully said. "What in hell do you want to go *there* for? Didn't anyone tell you about that place? Maybe I should remind you. It's a stinking village and a customs house, and nothing, repeat nothing, else. No regular air service, no train, you have to drive the whole way, 400 miles twelve hours on the road."

"Sure, everyone knows that," said Malko, "but I think we'll find some answers there, so that's where I'm going."

"You're crazy," said Derieux.

"I get it. You just don't want to come."

"Oh no, I didn't say that. Sure, I'd just love to go. After all, it's your money. When do we leave?"

"Tomorrow morning, about six if possible. Oh, and we have a passenger: the Belgian guy we met here yesterday."

"He's coming rubbernecking, I suppose? What did you have to tell him—that the Arabian Nights started at Khorramshahr?"

"No, he's interested in the same thing we are."

"I get it. Okay, I'll be there at six."

"If anyone wants to know, you could say we're going on an excursion to the Karaj Dam; you know, sightseeing?"

"Yeah. See you tomorrow."

Malko found Van der Staern in the dining room, moodily contemplating the cold buffet.

"Where the hell have you been?" he asked irritably. "Still chasing nymphets? I imagine you always do business this way."

"On the contrary," said Malko, unruffled by this display of ingratitude, "I've been working for you."

"And?"

"And I think I'm getting close to a—er—final solution."

Van der Staern looked more cheerful. He nudged him in the ribs and winked. "When this is all over we'll go to Beirut for two or three days. I've been told about a little place—nothing but blondes."

Malko smiled but did not answer. Van der Staern's high spirits would have been lowered somewhat by a glimpse of the late purchaser of his wheat. The old man had had *his* final solution.

They ate dinner in an almost empty dining-room. Dessert came, and Malko announced, "We leave tomorrow morning at six."

The Belgian made a sour face. "Do I really have to go?"

"Absolutely. I hope you haven't forgotten our agreement. You get your money, *when* we get back."

"It'll be absolute bloody murder."

"Sure," Malko agreed. "By the way, how's the wheat stored?"

"It's in railway cars. That's what worries me; this heat can't be doing it any good."

"What do you care now it's sold?"

"We only have their word for that so far."

True, he thought. An Iranian's word isn't worth a lot in a business deal, and a dead Iranian's word . . .

"How many cars?" asked Malko.

"Ten."

A tiny light started to flash inside his brain. Ten railway cars, and ten lines of code on that piece of paper.

He considered for a moment telling Van der Staern about the old man, but decided against it. The Belgian was hardly the warrior type, and he'd need a bit of kidding if he was going to be persuaded to come on this trip.

"Do you have any evidence of ownership, so we can actually get to see the stuff?"

"Certainly."

"Good. We'd better get some sleep, then. We have some traveling to do tomorrow."

They took the same elevator. Malko got off at his floor, and said goodnight. Before he went to bed, he dismantled and carefully cleaned the Colt, loaded it and filled two spare clips with ammunition.

CHAPTER SIX

Malko dozed, stretched out on the back seat. Derieux was driving the big Mercedes very quickly, the needle hovering near the hundred mark.

As far as the temperature was concerned they had a choice. They could shut the windows and die of heat, or open them and let the dust choke them to death.

"How about a drink?" Van der Staern's tongue was literally hanging out.

Wordlessly Derieux slowed down, and at the next village he stopped. There was a combination grocer-butcher-and-bar, and they fell with something resembling eagerness on the tepid beer and sour ewe's milk. Dry scraps of cooked meat described as shishkebab, were offered, and politely refused.

This was the real desert, the heartland of Iran: no telephone, no telegraph, even the railway had petered out, and in the rainy season the road disappeared under three feet of water.

Suddenly, as they rushed through this desolation, Derieux saw a black speck on the road far ahead. They got closer, and it turned into a man in uniform riding a mule. Curious. Derieux slowed down and waited. Evidently delighted to have a little company, the man rode up and started to chatter in Persian to Derieux, who listened, nodding, and then all at once started to laugh like a crazy man, choking on the dusty air.

"You know who this guy is?" he chuckled.

"No," said Van der Staern.

"A telegraph messenger."

"You're mad."

"Wrong. He's taking a telegram to a party of Italian prospectors lost in the desert. He's been going for three days, and he still has some way to go, plus the return trip."

"The mail really hurries in this country," heavily remarked Van der Staern. "Let's hope cash transfers are a bit quicker."

Malko ignored the crack. The Colt had been digging into him as he lay curled up on the seat, and he had slipped it under the seat. Before they left, Derieux had shown him a colossal long-barrelled Smith and Wesson hidden in the glove box. A guy with a lot of foresight.

Malko had had a bellyful of Iran. When he told Derieux about the old man and the dollars, the other had nodded and said: "This stinks. They don't get bloodthirsty like this unless it's really serious. Listen, the telephone may not work so good here, but the Arab telephone sure does; they may be expecting us."

Malko stretched. It was six in the evening. They had been driving like maniacs since midday, and now they were less than an hour from Khorramshahr. The heat was heavy, clinging, but the sun was beginning to sink below the horizon. That helped.

They were in the outskirts of the town. Yellow with dust, the Mercedes wove between flocks of milling bicycles, carts and taxis.

Derieux said, "I know a hotel where the air-conditioning works, more or less. It's called the Vanak. Also it's in the center of town. If you can call it a center."

The hotel looked like a converted railway station, but the vents of the air-conditioning did exhale an icy smell of kerosene into the rooms. Malko slipped the Colt under his mattress, locked the door and collapsed onto the bed.

He woke with a start. The sun was already high, and the unexpected noise that woke him was the rhythmic braying of a ship's siren, as an oil tanker left Khorramshahr port.

He quickly slipped into a shirt and slacks and went downstairs. Derieux and Van der Staern were already having breakfast: toast, white cheese, tea and caviar. Van der Staern was eating with a small spoon. Derieux said mockingly, "You wait and see what'll happen to your liver."

"You leave my liver alone." Then, to Malko, "What are we going to do now?"

"Do you have all your papers?"

"Yes."

"Then we're going to find out where the wheat's kept and have a look at it. After that, we'll see; it depends on what we find."

Derieux had a word with the owner of the hotel, who told him how to get to the freightyard, where trains coming from the frontier were stored.

They were there in ten minutes. Derieux assumed command, and Malko and Van der Staern trudged behind him as he toured countless squalid offices. No one knew anything about the wheat. In every office there was an official, and every time Derieux would explain the situation, slip the man ten rials and wait. Inevitably the man would nod his head and click his tongue, which is another of the Persian ways of saying no.

Some two hundred rials later they finally found a little old man who triumphantly produced a bundle of documents covered with stamps and signatures: the customs receipt for the wheat. It was still in the wagons, in a yard where goods were held before dispatch to Teheran, in the southern part of the town. Derieux gave the man a lavish fifty rials, and they left.

A faded sign directed them to a storage yard in the middle of the desert, surrounded by a high wire fence.

The temperature was about 120 degrees. "Can you imagine what state my wheat's in?" muttered Van der Staern.

An Iranian guarded the entrance. Stupefied by the heat, he scarcely glanced at the papers.

"Down the end. Can't miss it, 's another gate, you gotta ask again." He sank back into his stupor, his cap tipped forward on to his nose.

Derieux climbed wearily back behind the wheel and wound the Mercedes between countless sidings full of strings of railway cars. The place was deserted. Rounding a corner they came abruptly to a military guard-post. A sentry looked up, eased the strap of his submachine-gun off his shoulder and started to walk toward them. Derieux braked, and got slowly out of the car.

"We've come to see Mr. Van der Staern's wheat," he announced, importantly brandishing his papers.

The soldier shook his head. "No one's allowed in."

"Then go and get your boss."

"I'm not allowed to leave here."

"Then let me through and *I'll* get your boss."

"Ain't allowed."

And the muzzle of the submachine-gun became more menacing. The soldier was sweating profusely, and he was in a foul temper. They had taken him away from his goats to put him in the army, and now these men came along to annoy him. He decided he'd spent enough time standing out in the sun arguing with foreigners, and went back to his sentry-box.

"Why don't we just go in?" suggested Van der Staern.

"You want to be buried here?" said Derieux. "This idiot only understands orders. All we can do is wait for an officer to show. No, hang on; I've got an idea."

He went back to the car and started to sound the

horn, long, annoying blasts. The soldier jumped up and pointed his gun at the car, but his orders didn't include stopping people making a noise. Besides which he was secretly rather awed by this marvelous big car, having learned through bitter if narrow experience that power resides in the rich. He was, moreover, rather taken with the idea of his lieutenant being brusquely awakened in the middle of his siesta. He started to laugh, his teeth gleaming under the heavy black mustache.

Derieux applied himself to his task with increased vigor. Nothing. He tried short blasts, and then long ones again.

Someone shot out of a wooden building and ran toward the gate. An officer, his tie hanging loose, buckling his belt as he ran. He rushed up to the Mercedes, apoplectic with rage.

"Have you finished?" he screamed at Derieux.

"This halfwit wouldn't go and fetch you," the Belgian replied mildly.

"That's right! He was obeying his orders!"

"Possibly, but we didn't come specially from Teheran to spend all day sitting in the desert waiting for you to wake up."

He pointed to Malko, sitting in the back seat. "My employer is a very important person, and he doesn't like being kept waiting."

"What does he want?" the officer grumbled, slightly calmer.

"He's expecting a shipment of wheat, and he wants to see what state it's in."

"Wheat? There's no wheat here. This is a military store."

He turned on his heel, but Derieux called him back. "The wheat certainly is here, as these papers prove. Oh, and my employer is a friend of General Khadjar."

The officer ungraciously stuck out his hand and grabbed the bundle of documents. "Wait here," he said, and took them away.

Inside the car it was boiling. Malko got out, and thought a cauldron of molten lead had been poured over his shoulders. A bottle of cold beer danced into his vision, swaying seductively between the strands of barbed wire . . .

Van der Staern took a few steps, too, and quickly got back into the car, leaving the door open.

Derieux looked admiringly at the sentry; he was sweating great drops, but he was okay.

"If they leave us to stew here for an hour we'll die."

Malko didn't answer; he was saving his saliva.

After what seemed to be forever, and was in fact little more than fifteen minutes, the lieutenant came back, this time with a big smile. He lifted the barrier himself, and beckoned them to follow him.

Derieux moved the Mercedes gingerly forward, and drew up in front of the little wooden hut that served as a guardroom.

Inside, it was almost cool. They sat down around a table, and a soldier brought four cups of boiling tea on a little tray. Van der Staern groaned softly.

The officer smiled, and said in Persian, "Yes, yes, you must drink. You'll see, it's much better than a cold drink." They drank, burning their tongues, and, miraculously, in five minutes their thirst had vanished.

The officer scratched his neck and turned amiably to Derieux. "It's a real pleasure to meet you foreign gentlemen. We don't have many visitors, you know, Khorramshahr being a bit out of the way."

"Yes, well—"

"You speak very good Persian. Been here long?"

"Several years, but . . ."

"And you're in the wheat business?"

"No, not me; but Mr. Van der Staern doesn't speak the language."

The lieutenant now turned to Malko: "And you, sir, are you in the wheat business too?"

Malko frowned, pretending not to understand, and Derieux grabbed the opportunity: "Mr. Linge is an important buyer. That's why he wants to look at it."

"I see," nodded the lieutenant.

He saw, but that was all. He saw, but apparently he didn't understand. Derieux made the point a little clearer.

"You've checked that the wheat's here, I take it."

"Yes, that's right."

"That's fine, then, we won't keep you any more; you can take us to see it at once, and then we can leave you in peace."

"Yes, of course. There's one small problem, though—nothing serious, you understand."

"Yes?" They watched him, waiting.

"Well," he smiled very wide, showing all his teeth, "this material is under military control, you see, and to allow you access to it I have to have an authority from the Minister for the Army. It's just a small formality."

"Where do we get this authority?"

"From the ministry."

"The ministry? At Teheran, you mean?"

"Of course. We're just a little town here, we're not equipped for that sort of thing."

Derieux clenched his fists, but controlled himself. "You mean that we have to go back to Teheran to get a little piece of paper?"

"Oh, there are other ways."

"Like what?"

"I think the best thing would be to write. You'd have a reply within a few days, and meanwhile you could have a look around our beautiful country."

They looked at each other. The lieutenant's smile was candid, friendly. He had played an unusually skilful practical joke on them. Given the usual pace of the Iranian postal system it would

81

take not less than two weeks for a letter to get to Teheran and the reply to come back.

Derieux was the first to recover the power of speech. "Don't you think it'd be simpler to telephone? We really don't have that kind of time to play around with."

"Of course it would," the officer smiled; "but you see Iran isn't very modern by your standards, and here in the country parts the telephone doesn't work terribly well. Just at the moment, unfortunately, the line to Teheran is down. Termites, you know . . ."

"Termites?"

"Yes, they've eaten the poles and the wires for a distance of several miles."

"But surely," Derieux was getting impatient, "surely you're in radio contact?"

The officer laughed politely. "That's an excellent idea."

"But?" There had to be a but.

"I have to get authority to use it from my senior officer. Just a formality."

"I beg you to do so."

This had to be it. The lieutenant scratched his neck. "It's most tiresome. He's on maneuvers, and won't be back for several days. If you could wait . . ."

Van der Staern had followed this lunatic exchange in total incomprehension, but Malko had caught on at once. The man, like his stupid sentry, was obeying orders. That wheat was becoming more interesting every minute.

Derieux, not beaten yet, took another gulp of his tea, and returned to the attack. "I think perhaps we're getting off the point. The wheat belongs to this gentleman here, Mr. Van der Staern, and you can't stop him having a look at it."

"Of course, sir, you're absolutely right in principle. But, you see, the wheat doesn't belong to this gentleman any more. It has been bought by the

Iranian government, which is why it is here in the military depot."

"The government? But it was in the hands of a merchant in the bazaar."

"Perhaps it was. Presumably, however, he has resold it. Look, I have the papers here." He handed Derieux a bunch of documents printed in Persian, from which it was apparent that the wheat now belonged to the Ministry of War.

Derieux broke the news to Van der Staern.

"But I haven't been paid!" cried the Belgian. "This is robbery!"

Derieux translated. The lieutenant nodded sympathetically. "This is a very complicated situation. That's why I must have an authorization from the Ministry."

They were back to the beginning.

But Derieux smiled, and a thousand-rial note magically appeared in his hand. He idly folded and unfolded it.

"You would be doing us a great favor if you would come with us to the wagons, simply to have a glance."

The officer sighed.

"I really would be delighted to help . . ."

"And we would like to leave nothing but happy memories of our visit."

"Unfortunately the wagons are sealed . . ."

"That can be overcome. Seals can be removed and put back afterwards."

"But why," the lieutenant asked gently, "are you so determined to see the wheat?"

"It's a question of the quality," explained Derieux. "Mr. Linge has to know if this wheat will travel."

"Well, I think it can be arranged," the officer decided. "But not now. Can you come back tomorrow?"

"What time?"

"About eleven."

"That'll be fine. I'm very grateful for all your help."

"Don't mention it, happy to oblige."

They rose from the table with big smiles. The lieutenant shook hands all around and bowed deeply. Derieux left last. The thousand-rial note lay forgotten on the table.

"Well?" demanded Van der Staern.

"Let's get out of here," said Derieux through his smile. "I'll explain later."

They got back into the car. Derieux swore as he touched the burning hot steering-wheel. They sat in silence until they were out of the camp. At the gate the sentry treated them to an inpeccable salute.

"We've arranged to see the wheat tomorrow, discreetly," Derieux explained.

"Tomorrow? That's excellent," said Van der Staern.

Derieux laughed scornfully. "Evidently you still don't know this country. The Persian word for tomorrow is *farda*. It's the commonest word in the language often. And *farda* means never."

"Oh."

Van der Staern was surprised. Derieux continued, "The guy's already decided he's not going to let us get a look at the wheat, but he said it in the Iranian way, that's all."

"Then why did you leave the money?"

"To make him think I believed him. That way he won't get too suspicious."

"We've had it then," concluded Van der Staern. "We've come thirteen hundred miles across this damned desert for absolutely nothing! You should have got that authorization before we started."

"If we'd had it I expect they'd have asked for a bit of paper with the Shah's autograph. There's only one thing to do—go and have a look without their permission."

"Just what I was thinking," said Malko.

Van der Staern looked from one to the other in increasing horror. "No. Oh no. You're absolutely mad. They'll pick us off like rabbits."

"Not at night they won't. They'll be asleep if I know anything."

"Well *I'm* not coming," Van der Staern said firmly.

"Come on," said Malko, "you'll save us a lot of valuable time by coming to identify your merchandise."

"You didn't come all this way just to miss the best part of the adventure," reinforced Derieux.

Van der Staern muttered something; he still seemed unconvinced.

As they arrived at the hotel, Derieux said, "I'll see you guys later; there's a couple of things I want to buy for this evening."

The night was clear. The three silhouettes were sharp against the pale desert. The Mercedes was hidden behind a deserted hut about half a mile back. They worked along the barbed-wire fence of the military camp on the far side from the guardroom.

"Okay, that's far enough," whispered Derieux.

He tugged an enormous pair of shears from his belt, and slipped on a bulky pair of leather gloves. Several dull snaps later the barbed wire parted. Derieux went through first, having shoved the shears back into his belt and made sure that the Smith and Wesson would slip easily out of its holster. Malko already had his Colt in his hand.

A patch of blackness appeared in the distance.

"That's the railway line," said Malko. "Follow it."

They walked between the rails in single file. The camp was silent.

Suddenly the cars were ahead, a long line of box cars standing some way from the buildings. The

85

three men moved forward into their shadow. Pebbles crunched under their shoes, but no one came.

Malko came up to the first box car. He felt his way along, looking for the doors. They were fastened with a heavy padlock; but could he be sure that these were the right cars?

"Wait for me here," he muttered.

He followed the line of cars, counting. At ten the shapes changed; now they were flat-cars loaded with tanks and trucks. He kept on walking to the end of the train. There were no more box cars. Good.

He retraced his steps. Van der Staern crouched beneath the car, apparently more dead than alive. Derieux was keeping an eye on the camp.

"We have to open the first car," Malko said.

Wordlessly Derieux took out his cutter and started to work on the padlock. He struggled for several minutes, swearing softly. It stayed locked.

Finally there was a dull "clack." One side of the lock had given.

With infinite care Derieux and Malko started to slide the door open, producing a terrible grinding noise. They stopped. It must have been loud enough to wake the camp, half a mile away. But no one came.

They set to work again, inching the door open. This time they succeeded in keeping the operation almost noiseless. But an unspeakable stench poured from the interior of the car.

"What the hell's that?" whispered Derieux. "Corpses?"

"Van der Staern, come and have a look."

The Belgian left the shelter of the auto and joined them.

He briefly sampled the stink and said, "Yes, that's the wheat."

"That's the wheat! Must have been grown in a cemetery."

"No, it's just putrefying. Not so surprising, considering the heat. It must be germinating in the sacks."

The door was now wide open, and the smell was overpowering. The outlines of the heaped-up sacks were just distinguishable in the gloom.

"Tell me," said Malko, "can wheat be eaten when it's in this condition?"

Van der Staern shook his head.

"Even starving Indians wouldn't touch it."

"Doesn't it surprise you, then, that they paid such a lot of money for it?"

"Maybe the other box cars are better."

"Maybe. Let's have a look."

Derieux picked up his cutters and turned to the second car. He was improving with practice: this one went much quicker.

The stench was identical.

The third car was the same, and the fourth.

"No point in going on," said Malko. "Van der Staern, this is either the best deal you ever made or the worst. . . . Come on, let's open a few of these sacks and have a closer look at your de luxe wheat."

They went back to the car. Derieux manhandled a sack from the pile and threw it out on to the ground. He produced a knife and cut the string. Malko and Van der Staern held their breath. It was like a cesspool. Derieux overcame his revulsion and plunged his hand into the mass.

He groaned. "It's full of maggots."

He sank his arm in up to the shoulder and groped around.

"There's something here."

"What?"

"Dunno. Like a metal shoebox."

"Drugs?" Van der Staern suggested.

"Hardly. Here they tend to export the stuff. No . . . it's got a handle . . . and it's very heavy."

"Try and get it out," said Malko.

Derieux was about to reply when a searchlight

87

flicked on; it was directed straight at the box car that hid them.

"Shit!" said Malko.

It had all been too easy. They had been expected. A searchlight going on in the middle of the night wasn't a coincidence.

"Let's go!" he ordered. "We might have time."

They ran for the fence; they'd be able to get out if they could reach the car in time.

Derieux was already sneaking out when Malko called him back. "Get down."

At the same moment a burst of automatic fire rattled over their heads; a group of soldiers had worked around outside the wire to take them from the rear: they were surrounded.

Several bursts of firing followed the first. Fortunately the soldiers were aiming by guesswork, but one volley spattered the sand very near Malko, and a bullet ricocheted off the pebbles with an ugly whine.

"Make a run for the box cars, we can defend ourselves better from there," Malko said. "They won't bother to take us alive."

They ran, bent double. The flare was getting closer. As it picked them out a long burst rattled behind them: they were already flat on their stomachs.

"Shit, a machine-gun!" muttered Derieux.

The flare hit the ground with a sizzle and went out. They leapt to their feet and got to the first car just as a second rocket climbed in a graceful curve up into the sky.

This time there was no firing. But the light showed Malko a small column of soldiers coming through the gap in the barbed wire and heading straight toward them.

"We'd better open the other door, or they'll take us from the rear."

Luckily the sacks didn't entirely fill the box car. Derieux feverishly started to pile them up, and soon reached the door. It opened from the inside.

He pulled it open and at once closed it again, leaving a small crack through which he let off three quick shots with the Smith and Wesson. There was a shout, and a hail of bullets hit the side of the car.

"Bastards were sneaking up on us," he explained. "Now they'll watch out, they know we are armed. We better get organized."

In a few moments they had constructed a miniature blockhouse out of sacks of wheat in the middle of the wagon. Both doors were open just enough for them to see out. They fired together, to show that they had two weapons.

They watched the searchlight coming closer. It was mounted on a jeep. Derieux took careful aim, and put it out. At once the wagon was blasted by a great burst of gunfire. The wood splintered under the impact of the bullets, and the wheat collected the rest. There were several automatic weapons firing.

"What're we going to do?" moaned Van der Staern. "Should we try to make a run for it?"

"With two pistols against machine-guns? We wouldn't get very far. What we have to do is gain time. It'll be dawn soon, and they won't dare kill us then."

The three men crouched in the blackness, peering out into the night. The enemy kept a prudent fifty yards away.

There was another storm of firing. Flat on his belly, Malko felt the bullets landing all around him. He also felt Van der Staern's arm trembling convulsively.

Outside, a metallic voice spoke, making all three of them jump. A loudspeaker.

"Give yourselves up. Come out of the cars with your hands up and you won't get hurt."

This was repeated in Persian and English; then the firing stopped. Van der Staern sprang to his feet.

"I'm going. I can't die here."

"You're crazy!" shouted Derieux. "They'll shoot you like a rabbit."

Before he could grab him Van der Staern had clambered over the barricade of sacks and thrown himself out. He ran clumsily, his hands crossed on his head, crying: "I surrender, I surrender! I'm Belgian, don't shoot!"

A long burst of machine-gun fire opened up in front of him. The bullets hit the ground at first, then they climbed up his body. He stopped, seemed to collapse into himself, then took a few more steps, his arms hanging loose. A second burst shook him pitilessly. He fell heavily on his side. Derieux fired three times, furiously, in the direction of the machine-gun.

"The bastards didn't give him a chance."

"It'll be our turn soon," said Malko gloomily.

As if to prove his point a machine-gun sprayed the box car. Once more they dived for the floor. They no longer noticed the nauseating smell.

A dull explosion shook them. A soldier had taken advantage of the covering fire of the machine-gun to throw a grenade. At once the sack that Malko was lying behind split open and emptied. Instinctively he reached out to catch it and as his hand sank into the wheat he touched a long, hard object like a water-pipe. He pulled, and it came out of the sack.

It was the barrel of a machine-gun.

He thought of the writing on the piece of paper that he had taken from the old merchant's body. The first line read: 12 M.G. 42 6 B.Z. 20,000 C.A. 30. MG42. How stupid could you get? German machine-guns. 6 B.Z.: six bazookas. The wheat was an arms dump. No wonder it was so valuable; no wonder Khadjar wanted to lay hands on it.

Malko suddenly felt a great deal better.

"Man, we're sitting on an arsenal!" he told Derieux.

He explained his deductions in a few words, and showed him the gun-barrel.

The Belgian just said, "Better find the rest of it, and fast."

Quickly they cut open the sacks. In five minutes they were sitting behind a pair of machine-guns and a pile of boxes of cartridges.

Derieux exulted, "Boy, what we're gonna do to them! They sure won't be expecting this. If that poor bastard'd stayed we could've given him one too . . ."

"Hold it, there's something else I want to find. You know how to use a bazooka?"

"Yeah, I picked it up in Egypt."

Derieux emptied his revolver in the direction of the enemy, in case they were getting worried, while Malko dug around, and unearthed a bazooka. In the sack next to it was a box of four rocket-shells and charges to launch them.

In ten minutes they were ready. Malko had four machine-gun belts round his neck, and Derieux the same; and now he slid a projectile into the bazooka.

"Ready," he said. "How're we going to do it?"

"We'll make an attack on the barracks side. There's bound to be a truck in the camp. If not, we'll have to fight on foot in the open country."

"Right. I spotted a machine-gun on the jeep. I'll try and knock it out. Then we'll spray them and scram."

Each put a belt on his machine-gun. The dry clicks of the breech mechanisms were loud in the darkness.

"Okay?"

Derieux took careful aim. The jeep's outline was clear enough. He held his breath and gently pressed the trigger of the bazooka.

There was a blinding spout of flame, followed by a deafening explosion; the whole battlefield lit up.

Malko just had time to see the two groups of soldiers surrounding the box car.

Then his machine-gun was firing into them. It bucked in his hand while the whole belt ran through five hundred shots without a break. He hardly bothered to aim, sweeping the ground in front of him. The jeep was burning—Derieux had scored a direct hit. Several soldiers fell, and the rest scurried back in disorder. An officer shouted: "Keep firing! Don't stop!"

Derieux's machine-gun answered him. He sprayed each group with short bursts, then sent a longer burst after the group that was retreating.

"Let's go," shouted Malko. They jumped out of the car, holding their guns by the upper grip. Malko was surprised at how light they were. The MG42 had been developed by the Germans in 1942 to stop the Russian assault waves, and its lightness and high rate of fire were proverbial.

They ran more than a hundred yards, and not a shot was fired. They passed the burning jeep and came to a group of wooden buildings, where they dropped to the ground and inspected the lighted space that lay in front of them.

It was a sort of parade ground surrounded by wooden buildings. Their enemies were at the other end. They barely had time to level their machine-guns; an officer was rushing toward them, a pistol in his hand and a dozen men at his heels.

"Mine," said Derieux quietly.

His gun spat out short tongues of flame. The officer fell first. The others drew back, leaving several bodies on the ground. Derieux finished the belt and quickly fitted a new one.

"We've got to find a car," said Malko. "Keep going."

Several shots sounded behind them. The second group, that which had come from the outside, had re-formed and come up in their rear. Malko swung round and let off a long burst without aiming. The

92

harsh chattering sound filled him with absurd pleasure. Poor Van der Staern.

Bent double, they moved across the open space
and found themselves in a long dark alley with a
lamp post at the end; presumably the guardroom.

"You go, I'll cover you," said Malko.

He dropped behind a tree and waited.

Derieux ran. Behind the building they had been
in that afternoon were three trucks and a jeep.

A burst of fire came from the place where he had
left Malko. Derieux saw the flash at the muzzle. He
swiftly worked around the vehicles. No sentry. He
got into the jeep, fumbled for the ignition and
started it. He put the machine-gun down on his
right where he could get at it and let in the clutch.

Carefully he skirted the building and reached the
alley. Less than a hundred yards along it Malko
jumped up from the shadows and climbed into the
jeep. He had no gun.

"Just in time, I've finished my last belt."

"Mine's got a new one."

The jeep cut through the camp, with it's lights
off. Then they saw the gate. It was shut.

Derieux quickly got out and turned one handle.
The gate opened. He did the same on the other side,
and got back into the jeep. A man came out of the
sentry-box and ran towards them. He just had time
to leap aside to avoid being run down.

"I hope the car's still there," said Derieux. "We
could attract some attention if we have to get back
to Teheran in an army jeep."

On the main road, near the place where they had
left the Mercedes, Derieux slowed down. Malko
trained the MG42 on the house and jumped to the
ground. Derieux stopped and together they went
right around the house.

The car was still there, and there was no one
around. In ten seconds they were driving away,
leaving the jeep and the machine-gun.

93

They drove down the empty road to Khorram-shahr.

"We better get the hell out of this town," Malko said. "There's nothing else we can do here. They won't be looking for us officially for tonight's business; they can't afford to publicize those arms. Khadjar got wind of our trip down here and tried to finish us off discreetly, but he'll find it much more difficult for him to arrest us. We'd best get back to Teheran as quickly as possible and contact the Shah."

"Right. We'll go to the hotel first and then hit the road."

A quarter of an hour later they pulled up in front of the Vanak. A sleepy porter let them in. Malko took Derieux's key, and swiftly packed both their bags. Just the same he found time to refill the Colt.

Derieux was already in the lobby when he came down. He had explained to the night porter about their having to leave at once, and he had paid for the three rooms.

It was half past three in the morning. They stopped outside the town to buy gasoline, and then took the road north.

The first few miles were tense but there were no roadblocks. They had decided to drive back non-stop. Derieux seemed inexhaustible; after a night like that he could still drive all day. And they had a lot more to do in Teheran.

CHAPTER SEVEN

A bright red bell winked on-off and a huge Persian with a shaven head came through it, holding a machine gun that spat fire and flames. He came closer and closer, and laughed mockingly. His laughing, leering, contorted mouth filled the room . . .

Malko sat up in bed, sweating. The telephone rang and rang. He fumbled for the receiver.

"Yes?"

"Mr. Linge?"

"Speaking."

"Can you meet me in the lobby an hour from now?"

"Who is this?"

"My name won't mean anything to you, but I believe we have certain common interests."

"Like what?"

"Like wheat."

A short silence. The anonymous caller spoke over-precise English with a slight accent. The accent made Malko's mind up for him. It was a Russian accent.

He hauled himself out of bed and into a shower. It was mid-day, so he had slept for twelve hours.

The scalding water lashed his skin, and he thought gloomily about poor old Van der Staern; without him they'd never have found the arms that proved that the CIA's information was good: Khadjar and Schalberg *were* planning a coup.

Or at least Khadjar was. Malko couldn't quite bring himself to believe that the American was doublecrossing his masters in cold blood, knowing the probable consequences.

He must gamble just once more: warn Schalberg. If he *was* involved the warning wouldn't mean anything, because he'd already know about the previous night's events at Khorramshahr; and if he was Khadjar's dupe, now was as good a time as any to open his eyes.

Malko clutched a towel round his middle and dialed Schalberg's office. Malko identified himself, and Schalberg switched on the charm.

"You're wondering about your money, I guess; I'm afraid I don't have any news for you yet, but we're optimistic."

"Well, General, that's not actually what I'm calling about. I'd like to see you, though, as soon as possible. It's really very important."

Schalberg seemed a little surprised, but he readily agreed.

"Sure: why don't you come by the office at the end of the day, tell me all about it then?"

Malko thanked him and hung up. He'd know for certain in a few hours; now he could afford to relax a little. In fact he deserved it. He called Tania Taldeh.

Eventually he got through. When he said who it was she burst out laughing.

"I thought you must be dead; it's too bad you didn't call yesterday, there was a great party at the Massoudis, I could've taken you."

Malko said yes, it was too bad, and why didn't they meet today for a drink, after she finished work.

"Oh, it's very difficult; there aren't many places in Teheran, you know."

Finally they arranged to meet at five o'clock at a club called the *Belougette*.

The lobby was crowded. A convoy of elderly American ladies clustered round the reception desk,

© Lorillard 1973

Micronite filter.
Mild, smooth taste.
America's quality
cigarette.
Kent.

King Size or Deluxe 100's.

Try the crisp, clean taste of Kent Menthol.

The only Menthol with the famous Micronite filter.

and every couch was occupied by earnest business-men. Malko was concentrating very hard on a Swedish girl who simply had to be a stewardess when a voice said to his elbow "Would you like to have a drink by the swimming pool, Mr. Linge?"

He turned to face a man of about forty, with the graveness cultivated by senior Eastern-bloc officials. He was unsmiling but not unfriendly.

Malko said nothing, and walked toward the stairs.

They found a table slightly apart from the others. Malko realised he'd had no lunch, and ordered vodka and caviar. The Russian had green tea. When the waiter left he said, "I hope I didn't startle you, Prince Malko, appearing like this; you don't have much to do with us as a rule."

Malko smiled. No point in playing games. "I'm not sure what 'appearance' means, and I don't believe I know who you are."

The Russian gave a little bow. "Vladimir Mikhelayev Sederenko, third secretary, embassy of the Soviet Union."

Malko nodded. "You know my name, so—"

"Precisely; and I know why you are here."

That would really be surprising. In theory only two people had known about his mission: the President of the United States and the head of the CIA.

"You're here," Sederenko went on, "to inquire into a plot organized by the fascist Schalberg and the terrorist Khadjar."

"You seem to be very sure," hedged Malko.

"The wheat! We have been following it right from the beginning. So large a quantity of arms does not remain secret; what we didn't know was their destination. Not for the Shah. Not for your people either, you have more practical methods. And not for us." He smiled "That left few possibilities. You and your activities opened our eyes. We know what to believe now."

97

He leaned forward. "And we must act quickly.

"Perhaps you were not aware that our respective governments have concluded the agreement on the neutralization of Iran. The Shah has been consulted. If the fascist Khadjar puts his plan into operation he will upset the present balance of power. We should be obliged to intervene, which could not fail to create an explosive situation. Can you imagine the consequences if Russian tanks entered Teheran?"

"But these are the sort of problems that ought to be dealt with at government level," Malko protested.

"Of course they are. But your government can do nothing; Schalberg has compromised them, and he's too deeply involved to pull out now. So is Khadjar. This is one problem that can only be solved on the spot."

"And what do you want of me?" Malko asked uneasily.

"Warn the Shah. He won't believe us. Khadjar's been too close to him for too long, and you know what Khadjar did to our party here, the Toudeh. But he'll believe you; or at least he'll take precautions to prevent the worst happening."

"And you're certain that Schalberg's in this with Khadjar?"

"Absolutely. It was Schalberg who decided that the Shah must be assassinated."

That was news.

"What about the arms? What are they for?"

"To destroy public order, and give them an excuse to proclaim martial law. By the time the army realizes it's been made use of, it'll be too late."

"I see."

"You *have* to see the Shah."

"I can try. Is there any way I can get in touch with you?"

"Better not; I'll contact you. Remember: you must act quickly."

98

The Russian got up, made a stiff little bow, and left, a gray man among all the suntanned bodies and brightly colored shirts. Malko's caviar came. It was quite true, it really was the best caviar in the world. Well worth a revolution.

After lunch he went back up to his room and composed a cable for Washington. Now all he had to do was make sure it arrived. If it went through the cipher section at the embassy Schalberg would certainly find out. Malko rewrote the text three times, and finally arrived at an interpretation that he felt he could safely entrust to the post office.

He just had time to go there before meeting Tania.

The *Belougette* was an odd place, on the first floor of a shabby building near the great Avenue Takht-e-Jamshid. Inside, it was like the bar in old Humphrey Bogart movies.

Tania was half sitting, half reclining on a long, low couch against the wall. There was no one else in the room. Suddenly he felt very hot. She wore a close-fitting black silk dress, and dark stockings made her long legs seem even longer.

"I was just about to leave," she murmured reproachfully.

"You would have made me very unhappy if you had," he said.

The waiter brought them vodka and vanished, leaving them alone in the dark, hot little room. Somewhere music played very softly.

"Please," said Malko suddenly, "you must have dinner with me; I'll take you dancing afterwards, it would be so nice."

She shook her head. "Impossible. I simply cannot go out alone with a stranger."

"But you met me here."

"Oh, that's different. Here nobody can see us."

"Someone might come in."

"No one will come in; I have taken the room for the next hour."

Quite a secretary, thought Malko, who rents an entire bar for a date.

She went on, "But if you're free the day after tomorrow, some friends of mine are giving a party. It will be very amusing."

He smiled. "I'd like to come, if that's an invitation. But I hope we won't have to stay the whole evening talking to your friends."

"What does that mean?" she asked quickly.

He took her hand and said. "It means you are very beautiful."

She giggled. "You Europeans are all so charming. You try to seduce every woman you meet."

"No, not all. In fact you're the first Persian girl I've spoken to."

She giggled again. "All right, then; I'll see you the day after tomorrow. I'd better send you my car, the house is up in the mountains and you'll never find it on your own."

"I see; you're kidnapping me."

They laughed. They were closer now. His leg was touching hers. She didn't move away.

"Dance?" he said.

She smiled at him. He stared into her eyes, trying to read that smile, but it was dark and secret, and he could see nothing, just the dark, liquid gaze.

They were exactly the same height. At once she pressed against him, in a natural gesture, as if they had danced many times before. He held her closer, and she put her cheek against his. He moved his head slightly, letting his lips brush her neck, and she shivered. His mouth moved gently up to find hers. Her lips were already parted, she was quicker with her tongue than he, more violent.

Afterwards they stayed together, still swaying. He gently put his hand on her breast, and felt her

100

tremble under his fingertips. She drew away from him, slowly, her smile a little mocking.

"I must go now."

"You're in a great hurry."

"We'll see each other again. Two days isn't long."

Her eyes shone, and he thought he read desire in them. She was young, but not that young.

Malko quite simply wanted to throw her on the couch and make love to her. He knew she would not resist, that that was what she wanted. But he sensed that he must not; that a civilized man should not—or rather that he could not, since Schalberg must be getting tired of waiting. . . .

He gripped her shoulders and pressed her hard against him; wordlessly she wound her arms round him. Then they went quickly downstairs. They saw no one.

In the street she was again the well-brought-up, rather distant young woman he had met in the hotel. She gave him her hand for an instant, and got into a big black car with a chauffeur.

Malko's chauffeur sat in his taxi, listening to Teheran music on his transistor radio.

Five minutes later Malko was at the American embassy.

He asked for Schalberg, and was shown in immediately. The general looked worried. He pointed to a seat, lit a cigarette without offering Malko one. Then he said, very slowly and with a show of choosing words already well-rehearsed:

"Malko, you have done something . . . very . . . stupid. You're giving me a lot of trouble. A real headache. You know?"

Malko waited. Something had gone wrong. The general eyed him sardonically.

"Perhaps you'd like to bring Mr. Van der Staern's body back to the Belgian embassy yourself?"

Malko's cool returned. "Sure, why not? After all, he was killed by Iranian soldiers in contradiction of the most fundamental rights." He felt rather pompous now that he'd said it.

"Evidently you've forgotten how many soldiers you shot."

"After they'd had a damn good try at murdering us."

"I see. And what *were* you doing in an Iranian army depot at that time of night?"

"Checking some information."

"What information was that?"

"I imagine you know the answer to that as well as I do." The general said nothing. "All right, the cargo of wheat turned out to be a cargo of arms."

"So what if it did? You had no business sticking your nose into our affairs. You get A for enthusiasm, but D for secretiveness. You ought to have talked to us first. You want to know the end of this business?"

Malko nodded.

"Some time ago we found out through leaks that the Toudeh was planning to bring arms into Iran. We tracked them down and followed them right from source in Belgium. Unfortunately there were traitors in our service; hence the attack on you."

"Lieutenant Tabriz?"

"A Communist, of course. They needed money to pay for the arms, and we let them take it, rather than frighten them off. It was a small price to pay for laying our hands on the whole of their network."

"But what were the arms doing in an army depot?"

The general shook his head and ground out his cigarette, irritably. "Jesus Christ, you *can't* be such a damn fool. Listen: we re-routed them to the depot so that Khadjar's guys could 'clean' the sacks of wheat. That way the Communists would've been hit pretty hard, because they really need those guns; furthermore, they'd very likely have blamed the suppliers, so we'd be killing two birds with one stone."

"The soldiers seemed kind of trigger-happy; why did they kill Van der Staern when he gave himself up?"

"They had instructions not to let anyone near the box-cars; they thought you were Toudeh agents, taking delivery."

"And they couldn't take us prisoner?"

Schalberg allowed himself an icy smile. "I'm beginning to suspect you of a certain naivety, Prince Malko. Every Toudeh member we've caught so far has wound up in the cemetery; they're simply less trouble there."

Malko nodded. His theories hadn't lasted very long. Schalberg had an answer to every question, and Malko began to find him very persuasive. Suppose the CIA was mistaken. Suppose they *had* been taken in by Soviet agents? The Russians did want Schalberg and Khadjar out of the way, Sederenko had made that clear enough, and this would be a neat enough device for getting the Americans to lay it on for them. He decided to suspend judgement for the moment.

"Well, General, I guess I owe you some sort of apology," he said in what he hoped was a suitably humble tone of voice. "Maybe I shouldn't have tried to play it alone. I ran into Van der Staern by sheer chance, and I couldn't blow the opportunity of sewing the whole thing up. I guess I was wrong."

"That's all right, my boy," said Schalberg, beaming. "It's just a pity it didn't work out so well; especially for Van der Staern."

That wasn't exactly absolution, but he had relaxed a little. Encouraged, Malko went on, "Anyway I can start thinking about leaving Iran. In fact I'd probably have left today, except I met this girl and she invited me to some kind of Persian soirée which isn't until the day after tomorrow . . ."

103

The general roared with laughter. "That's right, you can afford to take it a bit easier now. But you'd better watch out for these Iranian girls. They're kind of wild, and their men guard them like hawks; you could find yourself playing the lead in an Iranian wedding if you're not careful."

"I'll be careful," Malko promised, crossing his fingers.

"There's one other thing: the Iranians are complaining about all those soldiers you knocked off yesterday. I've explained it all to General Khadjar, and he'll cover up, but you may be interrogated by Military Intelligence. We can't stop them if they want to, so if they do pull you in, deny everything. They'll have orders not to try too hard."

He got up and held out his hand, the bluff, broadminded soldier again. "Good luck with your love life. Oh, and try not to fall into too much bad company, like you did this lunchtime. You won't get anything out of those people but bad advice. Leave the problems to us to sort out; and tell Washington we have everything under control."

The office door closed on him, and Malko went slowly and thoughtfully down the stairs to the street. At the bottom he almost ran into a strongly built man with a fair crewcut and dead eyes—presumably one of the embassy heavies.

He was going to hail a cab, then changed his mind and walked a little way along Takht-e-Jamshid. He was getting confused. He had no reason, after all, to doubt what Schalberg had told him; this wouldn't be the first time the Russians had done something like this. He decided to talk to Derieux.

He was outside a hotel, the Sefid. He went in and asked to use the phone.

"Glad you called," Derieux said. "I've got some news for you."

"I'll come over."

Derieux opened the door himself, the hound of

the Baskervilles snuffling along at his heels. He led the way into the spartan sitting room, and fetched a bottle of champagne.

"We're drinking the best this time—French Ambassador's. But I've got a tip you're going to like just as much."

"Like what—war?"

"Better: revolution. I've been walking round the bazaar all day, and things are really beginning to move. They got itchy feet because they're calling a general strike for tomorrow; which is how it always starts. The mullahs are backing them up."

"What, the religious leaders?"

"Sure. Their story's that the government and the Shah are combining to undermine the peasants' religion, and playing the Communists' game. Which isn't very original, except that this time they'll have arms. Our arms."

"So who's organizing it? Communists? Toudeh?"

"You're out of your mind. The one thing you can count on is that it isn't them. Right now I honestly can't tell who it is, though. We'll see tomorrow, when the shooting starts."

"Great," said Malko. "Jean, you may think this is a mess, but you don't know the half of it yet." He described his meeting with Schalberg. Derieux listened in impatient silence, his right eye rolling round furiously until Malko thought it would whizz out of his head.

"If that isn't the biggest piece of cast-iron hooey since the Indians sold Manhattan Island for twenty-four dollars," said Derieux at the end of the story, "I'm the captain of the Mayflower. Listen, the Toudeh could no more carry out an operation as big and complicated as this than they could win a beauty contest. You heard it in the general's own words, they smashed even the suspected Communists so hard that they went right on and liquidated their neighbors, friends and relations. I think we'll find out something tomorrow.

105

"If we want to follow the action—which I guess you do; you do? You do—the best thing'll be to get close to the bazaar about six in the morning. We'll have some tea with a friend of mine and wait for the action. You better sleep here tonight; you never know, the Security police could decide to interrogate you tomorrow."

"Okay."

Derieux lifted his glass. "Here's to revolution and ready cash: the twin tits of Iran!"

CHAPTER EIGHT

A long column of black smoke climbed vertically into the blue Teheran sky. At its foot, in the exact middle of Meidan Eidam Square, just south of the bazaar, was an army truck. It was upside down. A ring of urchins scampered around it, throwing things into the flames.

The driver was still in the cab. The windshield had been smashed by bullets. His face was blackened, and it was slowly melting in the heat. Three other bodies were lying in the street.

Malko and Derieux came from the bazaar through the side-alleys into Khiaban Avenue, and stopped. They were in no-man's-land.

At one end of the avenue, toward Mesdan Square, they could see blue police uniforms. The police had blocked the street with their jeeps at a strategic position protecting the Golestan Palace and the radio building. Only by holding this point could they prevent the mob storming up Khayyam Avenue to the Embassies quarter, and from there to the Imperial Palace.

At the other end of Khiaban the dark mass of rioters waited, filling the whole width of the avenue. For the moment they would not advance under the guns of the police, but from a distance they seemed to tremble with tension, as if the slightest encouragement would hurl them forward.

Malko and Derieux crossed the open space at a run, and hid behind the wreckage of a telephone kiosk. The glass was broken and the telephone hung mournfully from its exposed, torn roots. The rioters had even ripped out the phone wires, and they trailed along the pavement.

"This stinks," said Derieux. "If we go that way some trigger-happy cop's going to shoot us, and if we go that way they'll lynch us. This is one time when being a white man isn't much of an advantage."

"That's just too bad. We might as well head for the mob, we'll see more, and it can't be more dangerous."

They walked, very slowly, up the avenue.

Behind them someone started shouting through a bullhorn. The police must have had their orders come through. "Go back. Go back and spread out. If you resist you will be arrested."

The jeeps started to advance, hood to hood, up the avenue behind them. Each contained several helmeted policemen with submachine-guns and riot sticks.

The front ranks of rioters started to back off. The jeeps accelerated.

"They're going to get it right in the teeth," Derieux muttered. "And we have to be in the middle, which is an unhealthy place to be."

Then the shooting started. An automatic. A long burst, then a series of shorter ones. Malko and Derieux dropped into the gutter. The shells whined unpleasantly close overhead. Derieux said, "I told you those police'd be quick on the draw."

"Look again. That isn't the police shooting."

Derieux incautiously lifted his head. The jeeps were wheeling round and pulling back in some confusion. Several policemen lay in the middle of the avenue, and others had abandoned their jeeps and were running back down the road. A fresh volley of shots pinned them to the ground.

The murmur of the crowd turned to a bellow, and then to a roar, and within a few seconds it started to stream howling toward the police, trampling Malko and Derieux unnoticed underfoot.

When the first wave had passed they got up and were at once carried along in the rush. Around them people shouted slogans, orders, questions, women screamed. One group was kicking the corpse of a policeman and hitting it with sticks. They didn't seem to realize he was dead. A few of the rioters held bricks and clubs, but there appeared to be no firearms.

Then Malko's eye was caught by a movement and he saw a man take a grenade from his pocket, pull out the pin and hurl it toward the police. Then he turned and disappeared into the crowd. The rattle of a machine-gun sounded from the north, probably in Ferdowsi Avenue. That meant they had several automatic weapons.

The crowd thinned for an instant, and Derieux dragged Malko aside. "We better not stay here, this is going to get a whole lot worse. The cops are on the defensive for the moment, but there's two tank regiments stationed in Teheran and it's only a matter of time before they get here."

"Where do you want to go?"

"Where we were before."

They ran. The alleys that led to the bazaar were completely deserted. Derieux stopped at a wooden door and rapped several times. Silence, then footsteps, and the door was opened by an old man. He recognized Derieux and smiled.

The inner court of the little house was calm and cool. Malko and Derieux sat on cushions and waited.

They spent the night there. Malko had come along mainly for the ride—he didn't much believe in the kind of revolution where invitations were issued in advance. But at about eight in morning they were awakened by the noise of the demonstrators running through the streets. They dressed quickly and went out to follow the crowd.

"I think we're better off here than outside," Derieux said. He was a bit calmer.

"What do they want?"

"I've no idea. Usually they're pretty quiet; once in a while they get excited, then they beat up a few cops and that keeps them happy until the next time. But they never kill anyone."

"You say they don't have guns as a rule?"

"No."

"They do now. Looks as though Van der Staern's stuff found a good home."

"Yeah, but who with?"

"Either the Communists or the others, I guess."

"What others?"

"How do I know? Someone's stirring it up, but Christ knows why."

Malko jumped up and started to dust off his suit. "Let's go see. I've got to know who pressed the button."

"You want to wind up dead?"

"We won't do any good sitting here. I can't wait for tomorrow's papers to give me the answer."

"That's a whole lot better than not being able to read anything."

"Derieux."

"What?"

"Why are you such a little ray of sunshine?"

Grumbling, Derieux clambered to his feet and followed Malko out into the alley. It was still empty. From the direction of the bazaar came the distant mutter of firing. Single shots and bursts of automatic weapons. Then several explosions.

"Bazookas," said Malko.

There was no movement at the southern edge of the bazaar. Two corpses and twenty or thirty pairs of ownerless shoes indicated that there had been some fighting. Several shop windows were smashed, and another telephone box wrecked. The PTT was taking quite a beating.

"Through the bazaar," suggested Derieux. "At least we won't meet any tanks. If we keep going north we'll come out on Bouzarjomehri Avenue."

They met no one in the labyrinth. The iron shutters were down, and the silence and stillness were unnerving.

The open air on the far side was filled with an ear-splitting clamor. Ten yards away from them some boys were hanging a policeman from a tree. He wasn't even struggling.

Malko turned away, horrified. Derieux grabbed his arm. "We better beat it; they've gone crazy."

They were overtaken by small groups of demonstrators; they quickened their own pace, to be less conspicuous. The sound of firing still came from the north; Ferdowsi Avenue was crowded with people heading in that direction. Now and then someone flung a rock through a window; the moneychangers and carpetsellers of that prosperous thoroughfare were going out of their minds.

Still hurrying, Malko and Derieux came to the crossing of Ferdowsi and Shah Reza. Wherever they looked there were demonstrators moving in small groups toward the north and west.

"They never came this far uptown before," Derieux remarked. "The Shah must be getting pretty nervous. Let's hope his guards can hold out."

"But what do these people want?"

"Ask them. Nothing, mostly. Maybe they're making up for twenty centuries of poverty and oppression—grabbing at things they'll never own. But they have leaders, and *they* know what they want."

Malko interrupted him. "Listen!"

Derieux listened. Below the thud of bazooka shells and the rattle of small arms he heard a familiar sound.

"Tanks."

They were coming from the west along Shah Reza. Instinctively Derieux turned to go in the opposite direction.

"Hold on," Malko said. "I want to have a look."

"This is a hell of a time for heroics."

"Nuts. The point is, that's where the bazookas

111

and machine-guns are; so the leaders must be there too."

Derieux shook his head. "You have to be crazy. No one in his right mind fools around with tanks. How much good are we going to do when we're dead?" But he followed Malko just the same.

They didn't have far to go. Near the Teheran Palace Hotel they met demonstrators running toward them, throwing away their clubs and stones as they ran. Beyond them a barricade of buses and overturned cars blocked the avenue.

Malko and Derieux went cautiously forward. They came up behind another barricade; this time there were men firing from it. Malko could see the slender barrel of a machine-gun and the tube of a bazooka. There was a short flash of flame as it fired a projectile. Then he saw the first tank.

It was stopped in front of the gates of the University, its turret sighting down the avenue. The bazooka rocket missed it and exploded against a tree. At once its two machine-guns opened fire. Malko saw the men in front of him shake as if they'd been electrocuted. Then they were still. The tank moved abruptly forward, firing more short bursts. There was another standing beyond it and to its left.

It picked up speed, and Malko and Derieux dived into the lobby of the Teheran Palace as it growled past. No one noticed them: guests and staff alike were lying flat on the floor.

Both tanks thrust through the barricade and went on toward Naderi Avenue. Malko looked carefully down the road. There were no infantry following up.

"Come on," he whispered.

Shah Reza was still as the grave. Not a single living demonstrator remained. The noise of the battle had moved to the east and south, but there was still a good deal of gunfire.

Picking his way along the pavement, Malko

worked his way up to the second barricade. The bodies lay where they had fallen round the machine-gun. The heavy .50 caliber shells had torn them to ribbons.

Malko leaned over the man still clutching the machine-gun pistol-grip. It was an Iranian, a young man. A bullet had torn his jacket, and a bit of green paper showed through. Malko tugged, and scooped a bundle of paper money from the torn jacket.

Derieux whistled. "Jesus Christ." He was surprised.

Malko looked at the hundred-dollar bills, and he wasn't surprised; he'd seen them before. They were as crisp as the ones he'd brought to Iran.

Derieux turned over another body, and shouted. It was—had been—a European.

It was the man Malko had collided with outside the American Embassy. His chest was patterned with dark red bullet holes, but the face was undamaged. He still stiffly clutched a leather briefcase, and a Walther pistol had slipped from his other hand. Malko wrenched the briefcase free. Derieux caught his arm and said, "We better not hang around here, the army is coming, they're dumb enough to take us for looters."

"You mean we're not?" Malko followed him obediently, still holding the briefcase. They slipped into an alley and headed north. A hundred yards further on they came to a military roadblock. A terribly polite officer asked them where they were going. Derieux explained about the business conference they'd been to at the Teheran Palace, and how they were on their way back to the Hilton where they were staying.

"It isn't safe to walk around here," said the officer. "I'll let you have a jeep."

One appeared; they climbed in and roared off up the Shemiran road. The troops were everywhere. At the Maideneh intersection were two Patton tanks side by side; there were several trucks full of steel-helmeted soldiers in Pahlavi Avenue.

The sound of fighting now came faintly from the south. The rebels had been pushed back on all sides, and their final collapse seemed only a matter of time.

The Hilton was pandemonium. The lobby milled with hysterical people. An elderly American woman rushed up to one of the reception clerks and wailed: "When's it going to stop? I have to know, my sister's coming tomorrow!" But he just smiled apologetically and turned his hands and eyes up to heaven. Teheran itself looked comparatively calm. But several columns of black smoke were rising from the city and a small airplane was circling over the Shah Rezah Avenue.

Malko took his key and they went up to his room.

The American's briefcase was not locked. It contained a thick wad of U.S. currency, and a piece of tracing paper folded in quarters, which Malko spread out on the bed.

It was a plan of the city, on which someone had neatly drawn a number of red and blue circles, and written notes and names. They were all in the southern part, and were clustered round the intersections of the major avenues.

"Presumably those circles are the positions of the armed groups," Malko said. "That means they have the use of at least—" he counted—"a dozen automatic weapons. Not hard to check."

He peered more closely. At the bottom of Khiaban Avenue, where they had been two hours before, there was a red circle and a name. That was the machine-gun that had been firing on the police until the tank knocked it out.

"That's why they needed money and arms, then. The cash was to pay mercenaries to lead the demonstrators. That was how Khadjar was planning to take power. Only it didn't pan out."

114

Derieux shook his head. "Sorry, that just doesn't figure. Look, Khadjar knows damn well about those two armored regiments of the Imperial Guard; they're permanently stationed just outside the city limits; they can be in action in two hours. You don't try to fight tanks with machine-guns and bazookas. I don't believe he thought for a moment he'd even get near the Shah."

"Then what *is* he after?"

Derieux shrugged. "We can only guess. Maybe under cover of the riots he's wiping out the moderates who could make things tricky for him later on. That'd be his style. The newspapers'll tell us if that's what he's doing—they're all in his pocket."

"Sounds impossible. Anyway, one thing's for sure, Schalberg and Khadjar are working together and they're working against the Shah. Presumably he didn't ask them to shoot up his own tanks."

"Nothing's impossible in this country."

"Yeah. Anyway, we must get to him and warn him about the plot. Why don't we go back downtown and see what happened to your car."

They had a lot of trouble finding a taxi driver who would take them. Eventually one agreed, but as soon as they got to the outskirts of town they ran into roadblocks. Every soldier in Teheran seemed to have time to listen while Derieux produced his papers and explained about the car.

The vast square at the foot of Ferdowsi Avenue was full of troops. A Patton tank was burning out in Lalehzar Street. A truck covered with a tarpaulin passed close by, and Malko saw the heaps of tangled corpses.

The taxi dropped them in front of the bazaar, opposite the radio building. The driver would not go any farther; you could hardly blame him. Malko and Derieux picked their way between the patrols, and walked through the bazaar.

The Mercedes was a pile of scrap. It had been

set on fire and then used as an anti-tank barrier, definitely not the intention of the manufacturer.

"Too bad," said Derieux, "you'll have to buy me another. Lucky you can afford it."

Malko grinned. "Sure. The Treasury doesn't know I got five or six thousand back. We'd better head for the palace now. You know anyone there?"

"Rhafa, the public relations officer. He's totally corrupt, though, you'd do better to go through the embassy."

"Can't do that, Schalberg has too much pull. I have to go to the Shah direct."

"Whatever you say."

They started to walk. There were no taxis.

It took them twenty minutes to walk to the palace, and when they got there they ran into another roadblock. There were troops everywhere; through the palace gates they could even see their tents on the wide green lawns. It took them another twenty minutes to cross the street. The little square in front of the palace was guarded by three tanks.

A gigantic sergeant of the Imperial Guard stood in their path.

"I must see General Nessari," Derieux curtly said. The man glared, and let them through with evident reluctance.

"Who's General Nessari?" whispered Malko.

"He's in command of the Imperial Guard," Derieux muttered out of the corner of his mouth.

Once in the garden they changed course and were soon being shown into Rhafa's office. He was a dapper little man with cunning eyes behind thick glasses, and a high-pitched voice. Derieux explained afterwards that despite his taking a great interest in his female staff he nevertheless found time to combine the function of public relations officer with those of cultural attaché and spy; his power came from the fact that he saw the Shah every morning, and his influence came from his talent as an ass-kisser.

116

Now, however, he listened to Derieux's explanations with every indication of sympathy, making rapid notes in Persian on a sheet of paper in front of him.

"I shall be able to convey your request almost immediately," he told Malko, "as I will be seeing His Majesty tomorrow morning. What may I say is the purpose of this audience?"

"Its purpose is urgent, serious and confidential," Malko said solemnly. "I'm here on a special mission for the government of the United States of America." In lieu of a fanfare of trumpets he brought out his letter from the President. The little man blinked and handed it back.

In a much quieter voice he said, "Why didn't you come via diplomatic channels, Mr. Linge? You seem to have an official mandate."

"There is a reason," Malko replied. "I think it will greatly interest His Majesty."

Rhafa nodded discreetly and changed the subject. Tea was served. He dipped his upper lip politely into his cup and offered Malko a well-cared-for hand. "Telephone me tomorrow morning, about eleven o'clock. I shall know by then. Which hotel are you staying at?"

"The Hilton."

"An excellent hotel. Until tomorrow, then."

A diminutive secretary showed them out.

"If you get your audience tomorrow," said Derieux when they were outside, "I'm shamus to the Pope."

Malko nodded glumly; Rhafa hadn't filled him with confidence either. "Let's go back to the hotel," he said. "I want to put the documents and cash somewhere safe."

"I know a place."

They had to walk three quarters of a mile before they found a cab. The northern end of town was peaceful, but there were trucks full of soldiers everywhere still. Derieux bought a copy of *Ettaalat*.

117

A banner headline right across the front page screamed ATTEMPTED COUP BY COMMUNIST RIOTERS.

The article explained that members of the Toudeh, armed with smuggled weapons, had combined with trade-unionist elements to try and force their way into the main police-stations in the south of Teheran. There had been fighting, and several leaders of the National Front had been arrested. The army had remained loyal and had put down the rebellion.

"Khadjar's done even better than I expected," Derieux muttered. "He's killed two birds with one stone. Look, he's prepared public opinion for his own coup, by underlining the threat of Communism, and he's eliminated the moderates who might have opposed him."

"It's a good thing I've got the money and the map."

"Don't kid yourself. I'll give you odds that that nice blond boy's dissolving in quicklime at this very moment. And he was the only real evidence we had."

The Hilton was guarded by a morose group of soldiers with a machine-gun. They eyed the taxi driver suspiciously, but cheered up when they saw the two Europeans.

"Wait here," said Malko. "I'll grab the goodies and be right down."

The room was as he had left it. He took the suitcase and went downstairs. Derieux had a taxi waiting. They paid it off three hundred yards from the house and walked the rest of the way.

As soon as they got in the Belgian picked up the case and disappeared. He was back in ten minutes—for Malko, three vodkas—later. "You can relax now."

"Where'd you put it?"

"There's a secret compartment in the bottom of my water-tank. I put your case in a rubber bag and

118

refilled the tank. So your dowry's under ten feet of water."

"Swell."

The radio spewed out a never-ending stream of news about the riots. There was more fighting. The telephone rang; Derieux listened for a few moments, then hung up and came back to the table, grinning. "Apparently they're using bulldozers to dig the graves," he announced. "Khadjar sure doesn't do things by halves."

"You think it's true?"

"I'd say it was on the conservative side. We'll never know how many people got killed today, and I don't see Khadjar telling us."

Malko went to bed at ten o'clock. A dull red light shone through his curtains; the light of houses burning in the southern end of Teheran. The red light glowed, and Malko slept the sleep of the comparatively just.

CHAPTER NINE

The telephone woke him again. The Russian, sounding anxious. "I should like to talk to you at once. I'm downstairs in the lobby, may I come up?"

"Sure."

Malko hastily combed his hair. Sederenko tapped quietly at the door, then came in and put his hat on the table.

"You know you're being watched, of course," said Malko.

The Russian smiled modestly. "We're used to it. What happened at your meeting with General Khadjar?"

"He told me you were plotting a coup."

"He's a little bit optimistic; I wish he was right. But I have something more urgent to discuss. Did you know that the Shah was nearly assassinated yesterday?"

"No, I didn't. What happened?"

The Russian lit a cigarette and sat on the bed. Malko sat in the armchair facing him. There was a knock on the door.

"That'll be for me," said the Russian. "Well—for you, really."

Malko went over and opened the door. It was the chambermaid, nervously holding a large parcel. She gave it to him and fled. It looked like a small sack of potatoes, weighed twelve or fourteen pounds. On a label attached to it was written Malko's name and room number.

"What is it?"

"Open it," answered the Russian, smiling. "From me to you, you might say. It's a present."

Malko tore open the wrapping. Inside was a bag made of opaque plastic, with a zip fastening. He unzipped it. The bag was full of flour. White, glistening white, almost luminous.

"That's a little bit of your famous wheat that we managed to get hold of," declared the Russian. "It wasn't intended for you."

"So why bring it here? The flour's completely irrelevant. It's what was inside that counted."

The Russian smiled tolerantly, like a kind uncle playing Santa Claus.

"Malko, will you do a small experiment for me? Take a pinch of that flour, just a tiny bit, put it on a bit of paper on the windowsill, and set light to the corner of the paper; use your cigarette lighter."

Intrigued, Malko did as he was told, lit the paper and stepped back.

When the flame reached the flour there was a violent explosion, and the window shattered. Malko jumped backwards. The Russian just sat, smiling.

"What sort of flour's that? You're not going to tell me that stuff's what we found in the railway wagons?"

"Not all of it. But a small part of the late Mr. Van der Staern's wheat is an extremely effective explosive. And what's more, it's made in America."

"In *America*?"

"Certainly. During the last war your secret services asked for an explosive that looked like flour, to deceive the Gestapo search parties. That's a bit of it. It won't make a very crusty loaf, but it'd turn this hotel into a hole in the ground."

"Why did you bring it to me?"

"Let's say, to increase mutual confidence."

"Where did it come from?"

"That I don't know, unfortunately. Probably an arms dump left in Europe after the war; I imagine the man who bought the arms just put it in with

121

the rest. On the other hand I know where it went. That bag was to have got on to the Shah's desk yesterday. It was supposed to contain a sample of the purest wheat of the northern provinces; part of a display of Iranian agricultural produce presented to the Shah as a compliment.

"An officer would have unzipped it so that the King could see the snowy whiteness of this royal flour, and the assembled company, together with the Marble Palace, would instantly have been converted into heat and light. There'd have been about enough of the Shah left to fill that bag."

"I don't get it. This stuff doesn't explode spontaneously, does it?"

"No. But the zip fastener was attached to this thing." The Russian produced from his pocket an object resembling a small pencil.

"A traction detonator," he specified. "Very effective."

"So what happened? And how do you come to have it?"

"My dear chap, I can't tell you that. We have several men in the Shah's entourage, and on this occasion they were useful to us. We knew something was in the wind, of course, but it's partly thanks to you that we were able to take action this time. You put us on a path that we had missed. If you were to look at the list of persons present at this touching ceremony, you'd see there is one missing: he had to beg off at the last moment. One may have one's convictions without insisting on the ultimate heroism."

"Not everyone can be so fortunate," Malko softly interjected, nettled by the Russian's sardonic tone.

"If one of our people delivered such an object, he would have stayed with it right to the end. In case there was an inquiry.

"Anyway, we were able to spirit this 'flour' away and substitute some of the more ordinary variety.

122

This bag contains the entire supply. Don't throw it out of the window, you may not have time to get downstairs before the Hilton falls on your head."

"Why don't you keep it?"

"What for? We're not terrorists. Besides this may help you to believe me in the future. If you have a future."

"Your optimism overwhelms me."

The Russian got up and crushed his cigarette stub in an ashtray.

"No, this is a matter of realism. You threaten Khadjar's security. Yesterday's little excitement is only the first part of his plan."

"What's the second?"

"To eliminate the Shah. But for us it would have been done yesterday. With the Shah disposed of, Khadjar would have a clear road ahead of him. There's only one thing in the way of his grand design: you."

"Thanks."

"I should like to wish you good luck. We will help you if we can."

Malko frowned. "What I really ought to do is take the first plane to Washington and explain the whole thing to the President. I have positive proof now. . . ."

The Russian shook his head.

"That would take too long. I know politicians. Khadjar is supported by a powerful lobby in Washington. It would take more than a few days to disown him, even with your evidence. By then it would be too late. There would be nothing left to do but to recognize his government."

"What do you think I should do, then?"

"Whatever you do, it must be done here. Go and see the Shah. Or prevent Khadjar from acting. Yourself. Before he stops *you* from taking action, permanently."

His hand was on the door knob.

"But I warn you one thing. Our Sixth Army,

commanded by General Kerensky, has been conducting maneuvers along the Iranian border between Tabriz and Babolsar. We take this business very seriously."

The door closed softly.

The first thing to do was get rid of the Russian's present. There was no way of knowing whether to believe him—the attempt had failed, after all.

Malko picked up the bag and felt its weight. It just didn't look as if it could destroy a twenty-story building. But maybe it could, so he'd better get rid of it. The best thing would be to bury it somewhere. But if his taxi hit something, like another car, he'd be the center of an expensive fireworks display. Suddenly he had an idea, and went into the private bathroom that Washington was so kindly paying for, and tested the lavatory. It was unreasonable to be so surprised when it worked.

He very carefully tipped a little bit of the 'flour' into the bowl, let it dissolve and flushed it. The milky soup disappeared with an encouragingly harmless gurgling. He repeated the exercise until the bag was empty, then he folded it and put it away in his case. A little bit more evidence; that would give the chemists something to think about.

Relieved to be rid of a present even more embarrassing than the handkerchiefs his aunts gave him at Christmas, he went down to the bar to unwind. There was nothing to do but wait for Rhafa to call. Maybe there would be some more interesting people in the bar.

He sat down in a corner and was raising a vodka and lime to his lips, when, right on cue, a waiter came up out of the floor and whispered, "Mr. Linge?" "Yes," Malko whispered back, irritated. "You're wanted on the phone."

It was the Russian. "I thought I'd find you in the bar. I forgot to mention one thing about that 'flour;' on no account should you throw it down the toilet. I checked with one of our experts."

"Why not?" The hair prickled on the back of Malko's neck.

"Apparently the organic matter in the sewers can produce an explosive reaction with it; the pipes will burst and the whole building will go."

"Well," said Malko, "it's kind of you to warn me; but you called too late."

The Russian laughed. He wasn't enjoying the joke much. "In that case, my dear friend, I recommend to you strongly to dine out tonight—and as far away as possible."

The line clicked and went dead. Malko hung up and went slowly back to the bar. The vodka just didn't taste the same. A door slammed and he started to his feet. Maybe it would be better for his nerves if he put some distance between himself and the hotel. If it *was* going to blow up, it might just as well be without him.

He decided to go to the palace: it would be more effective than a phone call. He had no trouble getting in this time. The revolution was over. In five minutes he was shown in. Rhafa was still beaming and affable. He regaled Malko for some little time with the beauties of the poetry of Hafiz, which he was engaged in translating into English. Malko tried to listen patiently, but he was in no mood for a course in Persian literature. Rhafa suddenly seemed to sense this lack of enthusiasm. He stopped abruptly and said, "Ah, yes; I saw His Majesty this morning, and I mentioned you."

"And?"

"His Majesty will be happy to receive you."

"When?"

"As soon as possible," replied Rhafa, a bit nettled at Malko's failure to be awed into silence by the great honor that was bestowed on him. "How long are you intending to stay in Teheran, Mr. Linge?"

Malko leaned forward and rested his hands on the desk. "That's altogether beside the point, Mr.

Rhafa," he said softly. "I have to see the Shah not next week, not tomorrow, but now. Do you appreciate that? I'm in a hurry."

Rhafa blinked frantically. "In that case, and because the, ah, circumstances are exceptional, I will do the impossible. I am seeing the King again this evening, and I will talk to him about you then. I shall try my best for you . . ."

"I'm very grateful," Malko said . . .

"But you must realize that His Majesty is so busy at the moment. If I could say what it's about . . ."

"That's out of the question, naturally." Malko got abruptly to his feet; he had had enough of this tricky little man. "I'll come back tomorrow at the same time—perhaps you'll have better news for me?"

Malko came out of the palace gates, turned left and headed for the American Embassy. He bought the papers and leafed through them as he walked. Each one featured on the front page a large picture of General Khadjar, the conqueror of the communist rebellion. The University had been closed, and a curfew was in operation from 10 p.m. to 6 a.m. The Toudeh was responsible for the whole business. All its leaders had been arrested, said the article.

The Ambassador kept Malko waiting for nearly an hour. He was very angry that he had not come to see him sooner. He was a little red-faced man, bald-pated, with pale blue eyes. A career diplomat. But by no means austere. He left the Embassy from time to time. For cocktail parties. He shook Malko's hand briefly.

"Robert Kilroy."

"Prince Malko Linge." The Ambassador didn't like the title, but he merely said, "Schalberg mentioned you. In what way can I assist?"

Malko produced his letter from the President, and while the ambassador looked at it outlined the present situation. His mission made it imperative

126

that he see the Shah; could the Ambassador help him?

Kilroy compressed his lips into a thin line. "The usual way is through Rhafa, whom you've seen, and Alah, the Minister of the Court, but they're never in a hurry. I can put a word in for you with Rhafa, it may do some good."

"Surely there's a quicker way?" Malko cut in.

"There are ways ... through General Khadjar, perhaps. If Schalberg asked him personally, he would make a special effort. He is very well placed, after all."

Malko made an irritated gesture. "If you yourself had to see the Shah inside twenty-four hours," he said exasperatedly, "how would you set about it?"

Kilroy eyed him nervously. "Come, Mr. Linge, that simply doesn't happen. Customs must be respected; these countries have protocol that you might find tiresome but that must be adhered to. I would see the Minister for Foreign Affairs," he added, seeing the expression on Malko's face, "and he would pass the message on. But I really don't understand why you are so unwilling to make use of General Khadjar. We are on the best possible terms with him."

"I have reasons," Malko said patiently, "for not having complete confidence in his goodwill."

Kilroy inspected him curiously, as if he had just announced that the president of General Motors was a member of the Communist Party. "As far as I am concerned he is the most trustworthy man in the country. He was primarily responsible for putting us back in the saddle in fifty-two. And," he added heatedly, daring Malko to contradict him, "I find him personally most agreeable."

Malko had that blind-alley feeling. He saw no good to be gained from prolonging the conversation, and still less from revealing the real purpose of his presence.

He rose and said formally, "Nevertheless I'd be very grateful if you'd use your influence to get me an interview with the Shah with the least possible delay. I assure you it's of the utmost importance. Naturally I must ask you to keep this conversation absolutely secret, even from your closest colleagues. This is a matter only for you, me and the White House."

Kilroy agreed enthusiastically. Malko hoped his remark about the White House had had some effect, but he felt if anything less confident than when he had arrived. He figured Kilroy would screw him up if he could. The two generals represented the established order, and Malko was an outsider, a slightly raffish secret agent with a bit too much power; a sort of jumped-up odd-job man.

Still, the Ambassador promised to call him the next day. He didn't sound too optimistic. Derieux was still the only person who could actually do something for Malko, so he grabbed a taxi and drove straight over to Soraya Street.

Derieux opened the door, the huge mastiff snuffling at his heels. Before Malko could open his mouth to say hello he demanded: "You sent a cable yesterday?"

"Yes, why?"

"It wasn't sent. Orders from"—he jerked a thumb—"upstairs. I got a friend at the post office, he told me."

That was interesting. Very curious. But it wasn't going to stop Malko spending the next few hours with Derieux's contraband champagne.

CHAPTER TEN

Stretched out on his bed in socks and shorts, Malko lit his last cigarette. Everything was going wrong. On the pretext of ironing it, the chambermaid had taken away his fine black gabardine suit and burned it; Malko could have cried, and nearly did. With infinite care and a wet handkerchief he had spent a good half-hour trying to repair the damage. But the trousers would never be the same again.

Rhafa hadn't been at the palace when he called. Malko was met by one of his lackeys, shaking like a leaf, who swore that Mr. Rhafa's sole aim in life was to arrange His Highness Prince Malko's audience with His Majesty. Certainly tomorrow, the day after at the latest. Tiny Alah, the Minister of the Court, was of course nowhere to be found. Malko sipped the eternal thimble of green tea and left the White Palace in disgust.

He had tried to find Derieux again, but the journalist was out for the whole day on what was mysteriously described as business. He tried to call the embassy, but couldn't get through.

So Malko had paced up and down his room all day, envying the lions at the zoo; they had bigger cages.

Night fell. He watched the first lights coming on in the city. He only had two hours to get ready before Tania's car came for him, he realized with horror; an agreeable period of relaxation seemed likely, but there was work to be done first.

He had just finished dressing when the telephone

rang. It was Derieux. "I'm downstairs, thought I'd pop up and say hello," he cheerfully explained, and hung up, without waiting for an answer. Five minutes later he knocked and came in, without waiting to be asked.

"I got some information that might interest you," he said at once. "Van der Staern's guns found a good home."

"Ah?"

"Some friends of mine just came back from Ispahan. They were in contact with the tribes that live in the region. And these tribes just took delivery of a batch of arms just like ours, and it looks as though they're expecting to use them pretty soon. While they're waiting they're practicing on caravans and small villages and so on. To the extent that the authorities were forced to string up one or two of them who were overdoing things."

"That *is* interesting, but so what? The guns had to go to somebody, and what happens in the sticks doesn't necessarily have anything to do with the capital in a country like Iran."

Derieux laughed. "That's an easy one.

"One: the name of the tribe I'm talking about is—wait for it—Khadjar; and they're absolutely devoted to our favorite general. Family loyalties are pretty strong in this part of the world. Two: fifty years ago the father of the present Shah disarmed them, on account of cutting off other people's heads was going a bit to far. Obviously they're only too willing to help their relative General Khadjar give the Shah a friendly push toward the exit, since by enlisting their help he gives them back their honor *and* the means to it. In addition to which they have endless opportunities *en route* to tweak the balls of all the other tribes, who tend *not* to have firearms. You read me?"

"Yes, it's almost as if it were planned," said Malko bitterly. "But what the hell am *I* going to do?"

130

"Oh, there's one other thing."

"More bad news?"

"Depends who for. There are rumors that the Shah's going to be liquidated very soon—in two days, in fact, at the gymnastic parade they're holding at Azafieh Stadium. He doesn't often appear at public functions, so it wouldn't surprise me if that's where the attempt will be made."

"Got any details?"

"Not a thing. In a place like this rumors are cheap, solid information expensive.

"It's an extraordinary situation, really. If *I* hear a rumor like this you can bet your life the Shah's heard it too. If he does nothing about it, it's because he hears this sort of thing twice a week. And one day he'll shrug off the wrong rumor, and he'll wind up dead. Mostly they're complete nonsense; I reckon nothing'll happen this time, the way it usually does.

"There's one strange thing, though. The guy that gave me this tip just sent his whole family to Europe. So he must think there's something in it."

Malko nodded. "It wouldn't surprise me. Listen to what happened today." He told Derieux about the Russian's visit and the bad joke with the exploding flour.

"I wonder who's pulling the strings behind this one?" Derieux said, half to himself. "They've probably done so much double- and triple-dealing that they don't know themselves.

"Look, call me tomorrow morning. We'll go and see that little bastard Rhafa together. I still have a couple of cards to play."

"Like what?"

"Movies. Rhafa's crazy about them—certain kinds, that is." He winked lewdly. "If you see what I mean. Sometimes he even takes part, though I'm afraid with more enthusiasm than acting talent. Anyway, I have some amusing evidence, and he knows it.

131

"Maybe that'll cheer you up a little. See you to-morrow."

Malko was not so much cheered as thoughtful and somewhat removed.

The insistent ringing of the telephone dragged him from his depressing mood. Tania's car had arrived.

He decided not to take the Colt. It was a social event, and he would not need the gun to take Tania in his arms . . .

The chauffeur was apparently a deaf mute. The car whispered along wide streets for about half an hour, and when Malko looked up again he was in an unfamiliar district of isolated villas in large grounds, and fewer pedestrians than a back street in Beverly Hills.

The car climbed a long, gentle slope; then it passed through a gateway on to a private road. It went on for another mile before it turned the corner and he saw the lights of the house.

Tania was standing on the steps in a slim, shiny, jade-green dress that she'd been poured into.

She gazed at him as he took her hand, and for once the golden eyes blinked: for what he read in the deep green lakes of her eyes was so specific that right away he wanted to lead her under one of the trees in the park.

But all she said was, "I hope the journey was not too tedious, Prince Malko? Do come in; I must meet my guests now, but I'll come and talk to you later."

Malko went into the enormous villa and gazed round. A silhouette undulated up to him, introduced itself as Tania's sister and offered to show him around.

Malko trailed approvingly behind her through the semi-darkness past a series of people with impossible names, men who bowed and women who held out soft or firm hands to be kissed, all perfumed, pampered and provocative in varying ways.

Malko docilely followed his guide round an enormous cold buffet loaded with plates, and almost ran into the back of her as she stopped in front of a slim, silent figure sitting in a deep leather armchair.

"Saadi, I believe you already know Prince Malko Linge?"

The girl leaned forward slightly into the dim light of a lamp, and Malko recogranized the exquisite cat's face of General Khadjar's daughter. "Of course. How are you, Mr. Linge?"

He kissed the hand offered him; the evening was becoming interesting, as the prospect of a difficult choice loomed.

"How do you find Iran?" she asked. "Have you managed to see much of the country?"

"A great deal—and all of it full of surprises." Then just to annoy her he said, "Unfortunately I haven't been able to do all I wanted; the last few days have been rather hectic in Teheran."

She spat furiously, like a little cat. "That was nothing, totally unimportant! A few troublemakers demonstrating a little more violently than usual; encouraged of course, by the Communists."

She was moving as she talked, toward the terrace. Malko took her arm as if to guide her. "But I understand there were many people killed."

"Communist propaganda. There was some shooting, but the soldiers were simply firing in the air to frighten the crowd."

"But I saw tanks."

"Also brought up just to scare the rioters."

It was clear enough. All those dead people must have died of fright. She was either badly informed or an even better liar than her father. Malko tried a less sensitive topic.

"You must tell me where you get your clothes," he said. "You're always *so* marvellously dressed."

Evidently he'd got the tone right, for she smiled at once and cooed, "I go to Paris twice a year; do you really like the way I dress?"

133

"I love it," he declared, and capitalizing on his success said, "Would you like to dance?"

He laid his left hand, holding her right, against the rise of her breasts, and brushed her fingertips with his lips. She pressed her cheek closer to his, but her body did not follow. She was being perceptibly less affectionate than at their last encounter, but Malko was enjoying himself; and he was beginning to bask in something of a rosy glow, when he was startled out of it by a voice saying, "Malko, I thought I'd lost you."

Tania was standing behind him, and it was the first time she had called him by his first name. He made a move to stop dancing, but she said, "Oh, please don't stop; I was simply afraid you might be bored." After a short silence she said, "I had no idea you knew Saadi already; well, I'll see you later." She turned and swayed back to the party. That was bad. He must make his choice now, which was sooner than he'd intended.

"How about a drink?" he suggested.

"What a good idea," she smiled. "I'd like an orange juice, please." He went in to find the bar. He saw Tania by the buffet, surrounded by lecherous-looking men. She saw him, and turned very slightly in his direction. He went back to the terrace with the orange juice and a neat vodka.

To his relief Saadi was talking to two men so he didn't stop.

Tania was still very much under siege, but he was in no mood for an extended campaign. He slipped between two of her admirers, saying, "Would you care to dance, Tania?" and at the same time drawing her irresistibly out of the circle.

"You are appallingly rude," she whispered, when it was too late and he had already got his arms round her.

"Me? But all I did was ask you to dance," he said in what he hoped was a fair stab at injured innocence.

"Giving me no choice."

"Of course not. You might have said no."

She laughed, but continued to hold herself away from him. Malko patiently set about nibbling her ear in the prescribed fashion. She stiffened a little, but did not draw away.

"I'm so glad I found you again," he murmured, "but when are all these people going to leave so that we can be alone?"

"What people?" she said, scandalized. "But they're my guests as much as you are!"

"How perfectly awful," Malko sighed. "And I thought there'd only be the two of us."

She said, "You're crazy," but she didn't sound very convincing, and he felt her relaxing against him. They drifted into a dark corner and he let go of her ear and worked over to her mouth.

Five minutes later she kissed him, as warmly as she had the first time. They stopped, swaying, among other couples similarly welded together. They clung more and more tightly together until he had to lean back to catch his breath. The beautiful green eyes were moist and shining. Her pelvis pressed forward, she was entirely stretched toward him, and he knew that he must take her at once.

Then some joker put on a rock and roll record and turned the volume right up, and the couples separated slightly. Tania danced a couple of yards away from him, moving her hips like a Negress.

The necking couples overcame their initial annoyance and surprise and resumed with, if anything, increased intensity. With the exception of one or two wallflowers and the intrepid cardplayers, everyone in the house was visibly preparing to make love—except those who were already so engaged.

Malko had had enough of the vertical. He hauled Tania to an unoccupied divan, snatching a couple of glasses of champagne in passing, and settled comfortably down to the next phase of the

135

evening. Tania was stretched out almost full length on the divan; this he celebrated by sliding his hand up her leg until he encountered, to his surprise and pleasure, a stocking top. "Stop that," she whispered unconvincingly, not letting go of his neck. He peered over her shoulder, and observed that her dress was held together at the back by an interminable zip fastener.

A servant passed close to them to take away the ashtrays. He did not even glance at the girl sprawled on the divan. He and a dozen others were perpetually circulating among the intertwined couples, removing and refilling glasses, wiping spillages, silent and immaterial as ghosts.

"I'd like to make love to you in that dress," he whispered, tickling Tania's ear. "What a strange idea," she giggled, and put her hand inside his shirt.

He had known as soon as he met and spoke with her that he would make love to Tania, sensed her submissiveness as a trainer senses the moods of his wild beasts, instinctively. This was not complacency, but a sixth sense that rarely had deceived him. Now that he felt her hot breath against him, he revelled in his victory over this wild girl who had seemed so hard to tame.

She rubbed closer to him, then kissed him and murmured, "I must go now, or people will talk. I'll come back soon. Why don't you go and have a little dance with Saadi, I think the poor thing's all alone this evening."

"The bitch," Malko thought.

On all sides couples were locked in anticipation and fulfilment, but their numbers were gradually diminishing—the house must have a hundred and fifty bedrooms. Malko peered around, hoping to see Saadi, but without success. Her father must be a deterrent to would-be lovers.

Tania came back. She stretched languorously beside him and kissed him all over. "You must be patient for just a little longer. They'll all be gone soon; and we'll be leaving too."

"Where are we going?"

"There's a little house about a hundred yards from here, where our friends sleep when they come to stay. It's empty at the moment; and no one will bother us."

It sounded perfect. Malko desired her even more, and she knew it. This time she did not draw back.

"I'll go first, you follow," she murmured close to his ear. "For appearances. Now."

She got up, went to the buffet and exchanged a few words with a couple who were dancing, and then went out on to the terrace. It was cool now and everyone had gone in. Tania stayed there a few moments, leaning quietly against the stone parapet, then the darkness snatched her from view. He followed her. At the end of the terrace he found a flight of steps going down into the garden.

At the bottom he followed a gravel path. He stopped to listen for a second, and heard the fading sound of her footsteps. He hurried to catch up, winding between tall trees. Abruptly he found himself in front of a building. It was unlighted, and he could not distinguish its size or shape. In a soft voice Tania said, "Are you there?" He took her hand.

They were on another, smaller terrace. She guided him into a stuffy room smelling of lamp-oil, then she let go of his hand and said, "Wait, I'll put on a light." In a moment the room glowed dully with the light of two low lamps with green shades. The room was small; the only furniture was a large divan, two chairs and a small low table. "Isn't this perfect?" Tania whispered. "No one will disturb us here."

She put her arms round him and kissed him violently. He drew her on to the divan, but she wriggled free. "You must not be in such a hurry. That

137

is not the Iranian way." She switched on an antique record player that was under the little table, and the room filled with reedy, hypnotic, Arab music. It seemed to flow into her, and her body began to move and sway as sinuously as the whining, trilling melody. Somehow the zipper of her dress came undone, and with a movement of her hips it slipped to the floor. She wore a black lace bra and garter belt, and very dark, fine stockings. Malko's mouth was dry. She came closer and rubbed her belly against him; he put his hands on her bottom and drew her towards him, sinking his fingers into her buttocks. She escaped with a twist of her hips. "You must be patient," she whispered. She drew back and with one hand unhooked her bra and threw it aside and stopped still. Her breasts were high and heavy, almost too heavy for her slender torso. "Now," she whispered, "now!"

In one movement Malko came to his feet and reached forward to grasp her smooth slim shoulders, then there was a rustling behind him and he was leaning too far forward to change direction and the ceiling hit his head with a silent brilliant explosion. Tania's body remained in silhouette in front of his eyes, he thought she was smiling, and the lights faded.

CHAPTER ELEVEN

His eyes opened of their own accord. They saw a tall black figure standing in front of him. Maybe he saw it too; you've got to trust someone. Now, what else could he do? He opened his mouth to shout, but no sound came. He couldn't do that. Then he noticed that something was jammed between his half-gaping jaws. It felt like a handkerchief.

He turned his head very slowly towards the light. His neck hurt. He was still in the room where Tania had done her strip-tease, but now it was daytime. He could see a scrap of blue sky through the half-open door.

He turned back to the figure at the foot of the bed. His neck still hurt, but at least it was screwed on tight again. It was a man in dark clothing, a Persian; he was contemplating Malko with an air of total detachment. That was good, Malko couldn't have taken an emotional scene. The man was wearing some kind of black silk pajamas, buttoned up to the neck. There was an automatic pistol tucked into his belt. He was smoking a cigarette, and leaning against the wall.

Malko thought about moving a little bit. He made the big effort. He could lift his head as well as turn it. But he couldn't lift it much, and it hurt. He couldn't move his hands at all. They were handcuffed to the divan on which he had intended teaching Tania the Austrian technique of love-making. His feet were tied together with a thick rope which was also looped under the divan. He pulled against his bonds to test their strength; icy sweat

139

trickled down his face and his head spun. Nauseated, he flopped back and closed his eyes and fell down, down . . .

He was jerked roughly awake by a violent shaking. The man in black was holding a bowl, and he'd taken away the gag. Malko decided to eat, to restore his strength—and it might give him an opportunity to escape. But the man had thought of that, too. He didn't untie him, but simply lifted his head and fed him like a child. It was a sort of very liquid purée of soya. Malko choked, and by a miracle kept it down.

Then the man gave him a glass of water the same way, and then he left the room.

Malko's mind was firing on at least two cylinders. He thought about Tania, for a start. That was an unpleasant thought, or at least a very mixed one. She'd really taken him, like a love-struck teenager. But he met her by accident. She couldn't have known he would get up and talk to her. So why this?

Saadi. His head ached with the effort, but it was coming. Saadi had pushed him at Tania, practically thrown him into her arms. That was supposed to lull his suspicions. Not that he had had any. And Saadi was the daughter of Teymour Khadjar, the man he was after. He had been taken out of circulation for a reason. Something was about to blow, and he'd be well out of things in this little summerhouse. No one would come looking for him. Derieux would simply think he'd stayed for a long weekend with Tania.

He tried to move again. The handcuffs allowed him perhaps two inches of movement, and the ropes stretched his legs painfully.

Just to see what would happen he tried to rock the divan. He hurt his wrists, so he stopped.

Three yards away the door opened on to the park. It was green out there. He looked round the room. There was nothing he could break and use to

140

cut the ropes. There never was, except in movies. And even if there was, how was he going to reach it?

A cool delicious mirage in the doorway. Tania. In a green dress of some light summery material. She floated over to the divan and kissed him lightly on the mouth. He felt the weight of her breasts through the silk.

"How do you feel?" she asked sympathetically. "Head not too bad?"

She was calm and smiling, as if she were bringing him his orange juice after a heavy night.

"I take it this is some kind of joke?" Malko tried to snap weakly.

She exploded into giggles. "Almost."

"So untie me, and explain."

She sat down next to him, but she didn't untie him. Her slim fingers stroked his chest, and she stared at them abstractedly, as if they didn't belong to her. She smiled. "You know, Prince Malko, I like you. I like you a lot. It must be your royal blood."

"Well you're restricting my royal circulation, so untie me."

"I'm sorry, I can't. And in any case it's better for you this way."

"Tania, why are you playing these games?" he said reproachfully. "You really set me up, didn't you? I mean, I walked right into it."

She leaned over and kissed him again.

"I wasn't acting. I told you, I really like you a lot. They asked me to set this trap. I did it only because I knew you wouldn't come to any harm. I'll untie you tomorrow morning, and then if you like we can take the car and go to Karaj."

"To Karaj? So you can put my feet in a block of cement and drop me in the lake?"

"You are awful," she smiled, chiding him for his ingratitude. "No, I have a house there. It's lovely

141

at this time of year. It will be quiet, and no one will disturb us, for a whole week, if you like."

"Do you know you're completely without a conscience?"

"Why?" she said, hurt. "Isn't that what you wanted to do with me here? Or was *that* acting?"

"No, it wasn't; but there've been one or two changes since then, don't you think?"

She wrinkled her forehead. "Like what?"

"Like I'm stuck here on this damn bed, trussed up like a chicken. That wasn't on the program."

"Sure, but it wasn't me that tied you up."

"No, all you did was bait the trap."

"I told you," she said crossly, "it's for your own good. *They* wanted to hurt you. Maybe kill you. I didn't want that to happen."

"Nice of you. Who's 'they?' Your little partner in crime Saadi?"

"Why do you ask if you know already?"

"You've answered my question. So why did you help her, if you were so anxious for my safety?"

Tania laughed. She thought that was funny. "You know who Saadi's father is, don't you? When he asks you to do something for him, you do it. Last year someone disobeyed him. He was found up in the mountains, cut in little pieces. They'd put him between two planks and sawed it up."

"So our—er—night of love was all planned?"

"Not when I invited you. But I told Saadi about you the next day and she said her father might be interested."

"I can believe that. And?"

"He came specially to see me. He said you had to be kept here for two days. It was very important, and you wouldn't get hurt."

"Except for a crack on the head."

She felt the bump and smiled. "You'll get over it. Tomorrow I'll make you forget it."

"You can untie me while we're waiting. Or at
142

least loosen these things so I can untie myself, then you won't be involved."

She shook her head. "I can't. Anyway it wouldn't do any good. You saw that man; there are three of them taking turns watching the door, and they have orders to shoot you on sight. If they don't shoot you the park is full of guard dogs that will eat you. If you get past them there is still a guard post on the road at the gates. Outside are mountains, all cliffs and precipices. Believe me, you're safer in here than outside, so please, be patient. It won't be much longer."

Malko sighed, and closed his eyes. He didn't doubt her for a moment. Khadjar was a cautious man, and he had arranged things well.

"Listen," he said, very gently. "Do you know who I am?"

She nodded. "You are Prince Malko Linge. You told me. Why—aren't you?"

"Yes, good, but do you know what I do?"

She shook her bad in puzzlement. "No."

"Didn't it ever occur to you?"

"Oh yes. I thought you were in politics, because you know Teymour."

"I'm not in politics. Tania, do you know what a secret agent is?"

"A spy?"

"If you like. Almost the same. I work for the American government, in the Secret Service. My boss is like Teymour in America."

"I see."

"Good. Now, you know America and Iran are allies?"

She burst out laughing. "Of course. All those dollars you give us!"

"Fine. Doesn't it surprise you, then, that General Khadjar should want to keep me prisoner, and even kill me?"

"Oh, you know, I'm just a girl. I don't understand politics."

"Listen, I'll explain to you what's going on. General Khadjar is a traitor to your country. He's planning to kill the Shah and take power himself, which would be very serious for *my* country."

She looked at him with interest. "Is that true, what you say?"

"Yes. And it has to be stopped."

She clapped her hands. "You're crazy. It would be great if Teymour was in power."

"It would? Why?"

"Because Saadi's one of my best friends. It would be very good for me."

"But suppose he assassinated the Shah?"

"Oh, you know, the Shah has many people assassinated too. But it would be very good if Teymour won, he's such a good-looking man. Can't you see him at the Golestan Palace, with his white uniform and all his medals?"

"Tania, are you putting me on?"

She opened her eyes very wide. "Not at all; why?"

He sighed. "You are completely amoral."

"What's amoral?"

"Nothing, just untie me."

"Please don't ask me to."

"You know they'll kill me afterwards. I know too much. You'll have my death on your conscience."

"They won't. I won't let them."

"Tania, you're a child."

She kissed him. "Not altogether. As you've found out."

"Then at least deliver a message for me."

"Malko, I can't. Teymour would kill me if he found out. Listen, I must leave you until this evening. I'm going to work now. Tomorrow is a holiday and we'll spend all day together."

Before he could call her back she was gone. He let his head fall back. Several minutes later his guard came in to check his bonds. They weren't taking any chances.

Malko said softly in Persian, "How would you like to earn a great deal of money?"

The man looked at him.

"It's quite easy. Just untie my legs—nothing else. Ten thousand tomans."

The Iranian sighed. "And the general would kill me. It is better to live poor than die rich." He went out again. In a country like Iran a man who turns down that sort of money is a frightened man.

Malko settled down to wait, and doze. Whatever he did it would have to wait for nightfall. When the man came back to check that he was still securely tied he might be able to overpower him and take his gun. If it failed he might get off with a beating. It was a lot of "mights."

He woke with a start. A car was coming. It stopped outside, then there was a murmur of voices. One was General Teymour Khadjan's.

He pretended to be asleep. A few seconds later the room shook to heavy footsteps. He was shaken awake, and he opened his eyes again. The general was standing near the bed, together with a couple of toughs.

"How are you, Prince Malko?" His manner was as unruffled and urbane as Tania's had been.

"Things would improve if you'd untie me," Malko said with as much dignity as he could manage. "I've no doubt you're aware of the trouble you're inviting by holding prisoner an American citizen who is also a government representative."

Khadjar laughed good-naturedly and fumbled in his breast-pocket for a box of little cigars. "Prince Malko, you have a sense of humor. I will indeed have you untied. But not yet. Later, when there's no danger of your trying to escape." There was something about his manner that was less than reassuring, and Malko preferred not to think about it too hard. "I must congratulate you," the general went on, "on your perceptiveness. You have handled yourself very well for a foreigner."

Malko watched his face. "Thank you," he said suspiciously.

"In fact you very nearly caused me a lot of trouble. If your ambassador was a little more intelligent . . ." he shrugged.

"And if your agents were a little more efficient," Malko finished for him. "That gag with the exploding flour was pretty smart."

Khadjar laughed even more loudly. He really was enjoying himself. "Bravo, my dear fellow, I have nothing but admiration; it definitely is high time we put you out of action."

"Would you mind dropping the heavy villain bit just long enough to tell me what you intend doing?"

Khadjar stopped laughing. "I'm going to kill you, of course."

"Well, General," Malko said, still smiling, "I thought you were a little surer of yourself than that."

"Come now, Prince Malko, I'm not a child. I must kill you—not because of what you know, although that's part of it. In a few hours I shall be the legal head of state of this fine country, and you could say nothing to anyone that would have any effect on me. And there is no such thing as revenge in politics. Besides, there aren't many heads of state today who haven't a little blood on their consciences."

"So?"

"It's just that I'm a very careful man. I am also your enemy, or rather you are mine. One should never leave an enemy alive. That's how one may be sure of living to an old age. It's just an elementary precaution. And I'll let you in on a little secret." He dropped his voice. "I like killing people."

He sighed. "Nowadays, you know, my work is altogether administrative. Years ago, I was a passionate student of human psychology, and I used to interrogate political prisoners myself. Now I haven't the time to visit my cellars." He leaned forward confidentially, and Malko wondered if he ought to feel privileged, hearing all these personal confessions. "And just between ourselves, most of the people we catch are complete imbeciles. There's no amusement at all in killing halfwits." Boy, that's tough, thought Malko. "It's very seldom that I have an hour to spare to spend agreeably like this."

"I'm sure," said Malko, "that you'll make an absolutely first-class head of state. If you get to be one at all."

"Oh I shall, I assure you," said Khadjar. "In fact, since it can't affect you, and, as they say in poker, you've paid to see—I'll tell you what's going to happen."

"Please do," said Malko politely.

"I have decided it would be both elegant and expedient to eliminate the Shah and his closest confidants with one stroke. I originally considered using a rifle with telescopic sights, but I have no marksman of sufficient talent, and in any case the terrain is not suitable. Also there is always a risk that something will go wrong.

"On the other hand I have had no confidence in small explosives since the German generals bungled the assassination of Hitler. So I have settled on what might seem to you to be a somewhat extreme measure. I am going to bomb the Shah."

"You're going to bomb the Shah."

"Exactly. Tomorrow he will be at a very big gymnastic display and parade. He will of course be well guarded, but that will not hinder me. I have a little radio-controlled airplane loaded with two hundred pounds of dynamite, and at the moment when the Shah takes his place on the platform it will fly down and vaporize him.

"You may be interested to know that the plane

147

will be controlled in this way for practical, not sentimental reasons. A pilot might lose his nerve, but a radio does not think. General Schalberg has very kindly lent me an excellent technician. We've done many practice runs and he's come within a yard of the target. I don't anticipate anything going wrong. In the unlikely case of our innocent tourist plane being spotted, there would be insufficient time for fighters to intercept."

"I imagine you won't be present at this party?"

"I shall be delayed by heavy traffic."

"And this dastardly assassination is of course the work of the murderous Toudeh."

"You are most perceptive. If they collect the debris they will perhaps find scraps of Communist leaflets. You will appreciate that after an outrage of this kind a strong government will be an urgent necessity, for the prevention of social disorder...."

"And if necessary there will be certain tribes ready to help you wipe out the Shah's few remaining supporters."

"Good Heavens, you know that too? You *are* to be congratulated."

"But tell me, General Khadjar," said Malko, feeling strangely like a reporter at a press conference, "the Russians will know perfectly well that their friends here have nothing to do with this, er, change of government—aren't you afraid that their reaction will be rather violent? I don't see your standing up to Siberian armored divisions."

Khadjar shrugged. "The White House doesn't want to see the Russian flag flying over the Persian Gulf. General Schalberg will report to the American government about the Communist plot to liquidate the Shah.

"This is why your own elimination becomes more than a whim, by the way; there will be no one to contradict Schalberg when you're gone."

"Well, I wish you the best of luck, and I look forward to seeing you in hell real soon."

Teymour Khadjar smiled without answering. He called: "*Ara!*" and one of the thugs shuffled in. He gave an order in Persian. Smiling sourly, Malko listened to him giving instructions for digging a grave.

The man went away again and returned shortly with a carpenter's rule, and solemnly started to measure Malko for his new home.

"I'm six foot two," Malko said, "and I like to be comfortable." He wasn't laughing.

He suddenly saw no point in wasting his energy in resistance, though he would soon have nothing to preserve his strength for. He wasn't afraid of dying: it was a professional hazard. And what could he do? Dissuading Khadjar would be rather like opening a tank with a nail file—the idea was right but the instrument was wrong.

He thought regretfully of Tania. If Khadjar had any idea of how to live, she'd have made a fine going-away present.

As if he had spoken aloud, Khadjar said amiably "Mr. Linge, my men are digging your grave in the park; you have a little time left, perhaps there's something in particular that you would like to have."

"As a matter of fact there is—an hour alone with our mutual friend Tania."

The General smiled. "I like men like you," he said patronizingly. "I hate people who live like lords and die like dogs, but you I respect. I shall ensure that your body is returned to your native land." He looked up as footsteps approached.

The amateur gravediggers were returning. They had been joined by a man in uniform, who seemed to be the general's chauffeur. Khadjar pulled a bayonet from his belt and approached the divan, waving the three men out of the room. They left, expressionless.

Malko watched him and the bayonet in his hand. Khadjar's yellow eyes seemed to shine murkily,

149

like lamps reflecting off a river. Malko kept looking at him.

He sat down on the divan and carefully unbuttoned Malko's jacket. His hands were slow and gentle. Then with the point of the bayonet he ripped his shirt open. The blade was cold on Malko's flesh, and he shivered involuntarily.

"In my tribe, in times long past," said Khadjar, "they had the curious custom of driving a dagger into the heart of anyone they suspected of being invulnerable. If he survived the test he was, of course, showered with honors. Do you think that you are invulnerable, Prince Malko Linge?" He gripped the bayonet with both hands and placed the tip against Malko's chest, positioning it with care between the third and fourth ribs. It began slowly to sink in. Malko felt sick, and an icy needle of pain flashed through his chest. The blade was sharp. An inch of it had already disappeared and the blood welled up around the metal. Absurdly, he braced himself and tried to struggle.

The blade bit again, and he grunted despite himself. Then there was a dull, soft percussion, and the bayonet seemed to take wings. It hit the wall and fell on the bed. Khadjar swore and reached for his belt.

"Get your hands up," said Derieux, "and don't move."

Malko twisted his head around. Derieux was standing in the doorway with a silenced Colt .38 in each hand.

"Get up and face the wall," he told Khadjar. "And let's not play toy soldiers, huh?" He cut the ropes that held Malko's legs with the bayonet.

"Hands," Malko said. "Handcuffs, we have to find the keys. What're you doing here, anyway?"

"Later. The key must be on one of those two guys in the other room. You—" to the general— "you go first, and walk slow."

He went out, winking at Malko; at least someone was enjoying himself. Three minutes later he came back, still pushing the general in front of him. He only held one pistol now, and in the other hand was a bunch of keys.

"Unlock him. Slowly." He threw the keys on the bed. Khadjar hesitated, then shrugged and unlocked the manacles. His face had no expression.

Malko got up with a sigh of relief.

"Stand against the wall." Derieux's voice was calm. It seemed reasonable to suppose that he would shoot without hesitation. He handed Malko his second gun. "You'd better have this, we're not out of here yet. I had to knock off three of the bastards on my way here, plus the two next door."

"Watch out, there's a third. He's out in the park, digging my grave."

The Belgian smiled crookedly. "We'll wait for him; I hate to waste a good grave."

He pushed Khadjar into a corner. Malko got behind the general and held the gun a foot from his back. Derieux stood behind the door.

It wasn't a long wait. Heavy footsteps, and then the door opened. "General . . ." said the man, and then saw the empty bed and stopped. He came quickly into the room, tugging at the gun in his belt. Derieux's Colt made a small irrelevant sound. The man stopped again and put his hands slowly behind him to the dark patch in the small of his back. Then he turned round and toppled over. Derieux fired again, and the body jerked. Another hole appeared in the shirt.

"And three," said Derieux.

"Time to go," Malko said. "Christ knows who we'll meet next."

"I got an idea. This bastard has his car here. We can take it and him too. I'll be chauffeur, you and him get in the back. If he moves, cool him off. You can do it quietly with these things." He patted the fat cylinder of the silencer.

"You hear that?" Malko said to Khadjar. Khadjar shrugged his shoulders. "You're a couple of fools. Even if you get away you won't get far. If you kill me, you'll get even less far."

He stopped for a moment, then said. "I'll give you a last chance. Hand over your guns and I promise you'll be safe; but I'll have to keep you for a few days."

"Cocktail-party talk bores me," said Derieux. "I figure you for pretty good life-insurance. Though I personally wouldn't pay very much to get you back."

They went out. A black Chrysler was parked in front of the house. Derieux opened a rear door and Malko slid in. Khadjar got in after him, encouraged by the friendly pressure of Derieux's gun barrel. Then Derieux got in behind the wheel.

The heavy car moved away. The villa seemed to be empty. The drive snaked gently downhill between ornamental shrubs towards the park. The gates were closed, and they could see a guard.

"Ordinarily," said Malko, "they would let the general through without any trouble. I think he's intelligent enough not to make any trouble."

Khadjar said nothing, looked nothing.

The Chrysler came to the gate. Derieux stopped gently. The guard came up to speak to him, his submachine-gun horizontal.

"The general's in a hurry," Derieux growled in Persian. "Open up quick, idiot!" The man came to attention, and started to say something.

Khadjar yelled, "Don't open, shoot, shoot!"

There followed a moment of general indecision, during which a number of things happened. Khadjar flung open the door and heaved himself out on the ground and rolled away. The soldier cocked his submachine-gun. Derieux tried to get his pistol out. Malko fired twice and the soldier let off a burst at the same time. Both shots hit him in the chest and he fell back. The spray of bullets swept the car, the rear windows smashed and Derieux grunted.

Malko fired again, this time at Khadjar. There was a dry click as the hammer fell on an empty chamber. Khadjar got to his feet and zigzagged off into the park, calling loudly for help. A second guard came out of the guard-house, some yards away. Derieux leaned the silencer of his gun on the sill and fired twice. One of the shells hit the man in the throat, and he toppled over.

Malko got out and opened the gate, then climbed into the front passenger seat. There was a big patch of red on Derieux's shirt.

"You hit bad?"

" 'S okay," Derieux muttered. "It was the first guy. I got one in the neck. Can't turn my head. Don't think it's serious, though." His hands were dead white on the steering wheel, and his face strained.

"I'll drive," said Malko.

"You don't know the way. We have to burn rubber to get back to town before Khadjar raises the alarm. Lucky they don't have any radio cars, and they're pretty slow-moving people, 'cause there's two routes we can take."

"Where do you want to go?"

"Underground. First we've got to get to cover. Khadjar'll want us caught dead or alive."

"You don't know the half of it." Malko explained Khadjar's plans. Derieux listened, nodding, his face tight and his foot on the floorboard. They came into the outskirts of Teheran, passed the Darban Hotel and came on to Pahlavi Avenue.

"They'll certainly shoot on sight, then," said Derieux. "We'd better get out of the country before he takes power. Best thing would be to slip into Russia via the Caspian."

"But Khadjar mustn't take power," Malko said. "That'd be a world catastrophe."

Derieux coughed with pain—he must have moved too sharply—and said, "For Christ's sake, I'm bleeding like a pig; if I don't get to a doctor I'll

153

probably bleed to death. And I don't know what *you* have in mind, but by tonight every cop in Teheran will have your picture. And you'd better believe there are plenty of people at the palace, the embassy and the hotel who'd shoot you on sight."

Malko made no answer. It was all true. No one would doubt Khadjar and Schalberg. He was outside the law. He sank back into his thoughts as Derieux raced through the town, overtaking all the way. A policeman saw them and stopped the traffic with an imperative blast on his whistle, signalling Derieux to go through. "This gets better all the time," he said derisively. "They know the car. Any minute we'll get a motorcycle escort—all the way to the morgue."

He turned down a rapid succession of narrow side-streets, and then pulled up. "We better leave the car here, it's too conspicuous. We don't have far to walk."

He got out of the car, and stumbled and nearly fell. He leaned against the wing and spat. "That bastard really got me," he said. Malko took his arm, and a long trickle of blood ran down his sleeve. They hobbled, limping and leaning, for a couple of hundred yards, then the street became a cul-de-sac, stinking of garbage. Derieux knocked on a wooden door, twice, then five times.

In a minute it opened a few inches, and a little wrinkled old woman peered out suspiciously.

"Is the doctor there?" he asked in Persian. She nodded and let them into a small room with a beaten-earth floor.

In a minute a little bent man came in. Ignoring Malko, he squatted in front of Derieux and carefully took off his shirt.

"It's not good," the doctor said quietly in French. "I must operate at once, the bullet is still inside. You'll be all right down below."

He got up and moved the table. There was a ring in the floor that had been hidden by the table-leg.

154

He bent down and pulled and opened a trapdoor, with a ladder leading down into a black pit. Malko leaned over the edge and inhaled a strong medical smell. A light appeared in the basement and the doctor climbed up again. "Give me a hand," he said. Together they supported the Belgian's thick heavy body while he slid uncomfortably down the rungs. Malko went down last. At the foot of the ladder was a room, much cleaner than the one above, and furnished as an operating room with oxygen-bottles standing in the corner. Derieux stretched painfully out on one of the two blanket-covered operating tables.

The doctor produced a hypodermic needle and gave him an injection in the arm. "A little morphine won't do you any harm," he murmured. "I shall have to send out for antibiotics."

He climbed up the ladder and lowered the trapdoor. Malko sat down next to Derieux. "Who is this guy? Is he safe?"

"He's safe. He was Mossadegh's doctor, and he hates Khadjar's guts. There's a price on his head. This is the guy who does abortions for all the society girls and tarts in Teheran."

The morphine was taking effect. Malko took the opportunity to ask the burning question. "All right, so tell me, how'd you get me out of all that?"

Derieux grinned. "A spot of luck and your incredible charm. I passed by your hotel this afternoon, and they said you weren't back yet. I knew you were going to a party yesterday evening, and you told me the chick's name. I have some kind girl friends who helped me trace her. I went to see her at her office lunchtime, asked about you; she told me some crap about you leaving early. The doll was in town, so you presumably weren't at an orgy in the country, so I thought I'd better have a look. I took a taxi and my guns and I came. I had a little trouble in the park on account of the heavies. Lucky they didn't all come at once. Then this guy pointed a submachine-gun at me and I figured I was on the right track. That was the guy outside your room."

"And what happened?"

"He forgot to cock it. The silencer helped, after that. It's nice the way those things don't disturb people."

The ladder shook, and the doctor came down it with an armful of bottles and boxes.

"I'd rather you went upstairs during the operation," he said to Malko. That suited Malko too. He climbed out and sat on a box.

Three quarters of an hour later the doctor climbed back into the room. His sleeves were rolled up and his face shining with sweat. "Finished," he said. "He'll be okay, but I can't let you move him for a week. I'll keep him downstairs. You can see him now."

Malko went down. Derieux was sitting up on the couch, naked to the waist, smoking a cigarette. Bandages covered his left shoulder and neck. In a saucer on a small table was a misshapen scrap of lead—the bullet that had been inside him.

"This doc's the king," he announced cheerfully. "Didn't feel a thing. But when we try to get out of this place things are going to be pretty tricky. Iran's finished as far as I'm concerned."

Malko frowned. "I'm not finished yet. I'll try one more time tomorrow—I'll go to see the Ambassador again."

"You're crazy. Khadjar's already set the wheels in motion. That's the dumbest way to get yourself killed I ever heard of."

"I have to do it. No one can stop this assassination except me."

"Yeah," said Derieux sceptically. "Do what you want. I'd lay about a million to one against. Anyway, you'd better get some rest tonight."

He was right about that.

Malko stretched out fully dressed on the other couch after the doctor bandaged his chest. He was asleep before he knew it. Tomorrow would be a long day.

CHAPTER TWELVE

Now he knew what it felt like to be hunted. For one thing, he felt unbelievably dirty. He caught sight of his reflection in a carpet-merchant's window; his jaw was unshaven and his shirt torn and dirty, and he looked like the average Iranian. Derieux's hideout was secure, but it was short on modern amenities.

There weren't many other Europeans in the street; that was worrying, it made him easier to spot; Khadjar would certainly have set his heavies on Malko's trail by now.

A jeep full of armed police roared by, but they didn't even glance in his direction, which compensated for the unwashed feeling. At Ferdowsi and Shah Reza huge banners celebrated the Shah's birthday and announced the gymnastic display and parade at Azafieh Stadium.

It was becoming clear that Khadjar and Schalberg would kill the Shah that afternoon; nothing could stop them now. The plan was simple. The Shah and everyone around him would be atomized by so much high explosive—taking power would be a formality. And Malko would presumably suffer a fatal accident before he could get out of the country, followed by polite apologies to the American government for the clumsiness of the Iranian police.

That was what made his job a bad one: he didn't want to get killed, ignominiously, out in a place like this—wrong, hostile, unfamiliar. He had to keep trying, but on foot in the wide avenue he felt naked and defenseless.

He looked at his watch. It was midday. The parade was due to begin at two o'clock. The assassination would certainly be in the beginning, not later than two-thirty.

He ought to have a car, so at least he'd be able to get around. That made him feel more cheerful, having a practical problem to solve.

He had just walked past the Park Hotel. He walked the hundred yards back to it, and went into the courtyard.

It was a holiday, and the businessmen staying at the hotel weren't doing any business, so there were a dozen limousines standing idle while their drivers dozed or read the paper. Malko picked out a clean-looking late-model black Chevrolet.

He went into the hotel and headed for the bar. It was empty. He went back to the reception desk and asked the plump, smiling telephone girl to get him the American Ambassador's private number.

"*Befar me,*" said someone at the other end of the line.

Malko asked to talk to the Ambassador. Personally.

The servant went to ask, and then came back and said, "His Excellency will come in a minute." Malko waited.

"Kilroy here," said a male voice.

"This is Prince Malko Linge, Your Excellency. I must talk to you urgently. May I come at once?"

The Ambassador gave a sigh of genteel exasperation. "Now look, in exactly five minutes I'll be leaving for the Shah's reception, and I simply don't have the time to discuss your problems. I know you're in trouble, but I take the view that this is your own fault. General Khadjar's issued a warrant for your arrest, and from what I hear he has every justification. If you think you can go round with hired killers trying to murder important people and expect me to protect you, you're crazy. In fact, I'm not so sure you aren't crazy. Mr. Linge, just give yourself up, and then I'll see what I can do."

Malko listened in incredulous silence. "Your Excellency, I want to make it clear right now that it was Khadjar who nearly murdered *me*. I am on a secret mission for the President of the United States—or didn't I explain that plainly enough?" He was almost shouting.

"Indeed you did," the Ambassador admitted, "but—"

"And didn't I show you my letter, signed by the President?"

"Why yes, but—"

"Good. I'm glad that's clear. Those papers authorize me to demand help from any functionary of the American government. Are you somehow excluded from that category?"

"Of course, of course, but I have no power to protect you from the laws of this country. Especially where the matter concerns so good a friend of the United States as General Khadjar."

Evidently Schalberg had got his two bits' worth in here.

"All right, we won't talk about that for the moment. Right now I must ask—I must order you in the name of the President to contact the Shah *at once* and warn him that an attempt will be made on his life today."

"An assassination attempt? What kind? Do you realize that the Shah is even better guarded than our President?"

"I'm sorry, I can't tell you any more for the moment, but I can assure you that this attempt will succeed if something isn't done about it." It sounded a bit lame, but he could hardly tip off Khadjar. The general was smart enough to postpone the attack as soon as he discovered that it had been blown. And that would be that.

"Listen," the Ambassador said impatiently,

"we've already talked about this. I don't doubt your sincerity, but you must admit, secret agents have been known to make mistakes. I took this matter up again with General Schalberg less than forty-eight hours ago. The general's been with the CIA for twenty years, and his opinion ought to be worth something.

"He has positively assured me that there is no foundation in these rumors of plots and assassinations; they're put about by the Communists to create a state of tension. That's his considered opinion; Schalberg's no fool, and he's an expert on the subject. Furthermore he works very closely with General Khadjar, who knows about everything that goes on in this country. I'm more than happy to take the words of Generals Schalberg and Khadjar. But I'm afraid that you've allowed yourself to be fooled by the Communists; Schalberg told me about your meeting members of the Russian Embassy staff. I'm not going to go to the Shah with a story like this just to get myself laughed at, believe me."

"Your Excellency," said Malko very distinctly. "What would you say to a nice little job at the embassy at Ulan Bator?"

"Outer Mongolia? Why?"

"Because that, in *my* considered opinion, is all that you're fit for. And if I'm still alive this evening, that's where you'll wind up." Malko hung up. He had got absolutely nowhere, and wasted ten valuable minutes.

The plump little telephone girl was still smiling at him.

He said, "I'd like to place a call to the United States."

"Wait one minute, please, I'll see when the lines will be free." She tinkered with her switchboard for a minute, and then launched into a long conversation with the exchange. Then she turned to Malko and said, "I'm sorry, sir, there aren't any lines today. If you give me your room number I can try tomorrow morning."

Malko shook his head. "Too bad. Forget it, thanks anyway."

He left the lobby. The black Chevrolet was still there. He was beginning to think of it as an old friend. He went over, and the driver leapt out with a big happy smile. "I'd like to hire your car," Malko said. "Does it go all right?"

The man enthusiastically assured him that yes, it went very well.

"Good. Will you get my bags, please. They're with the porter."

Malko waited until the driver had rushed into the hotel, then opened the door and slid behind the wheel. The key was in the ignition.

The driver came out of the hotel just in time to see Malko turn into Hafez Avenue. He stood still for one uncomprehending second, then scampered yelling down the road in pursuit. The other drivers stared in astonishment. Even at the Park Hotel, where many strange things happen, they had never seen a customer steal a car.

There wasn't much traffic, and he drove fast along the Shemiran road. He made a left turn and then cut very quickly through several side-streets, coming out a little further down Takht-e-Jamshid, and parked the car.

He sat in the back, pretending he was waiting for his chauffeur, lit a cigarette and thought. It was one o'clock. In sixty minutes the Shah's armorplated Rolls Royce would drive up to the stadium at Azafieh.

If he could get to talk to the Shah he'd certainly be listened to; the ruler of a country like Iran must soon develop a sixth sense about danger. But once he was inside the stadium, Malko would never reach him: Khadjar's men would be everywhere, and anyone trying to get near the Shah would be shot the way you swat a fly. That would suit everyone. So he had to intercept the Shah outside the stadium. If he physically stopped the Rolls with his own car he might be able to get the Shah's attention before the bodyguard started shooting. The odds were probably not more than ten thousand to one against. He restarted the Chevrolet and headed for Saadabad, the summer palace. It was on the Shemiran road, higher up than the Hilton; the Shah would presumably leave by the main gate, opposite the Darband Hotel.

The palace was deserted when he arrived. Two sentries with submachine-guns mounted guard at the high wrought-iron gate. There were others in the guardroom. He went down the road again to check the other gate. Same story. Then he went back to the little square in front of the Darband and parked close to it, next to the river, as if he were waiting for someone to come out of the hotel. The road ended there. It was a bright day, but at that altitude it was cool.

He looked at his watch again. One-fifteen. He was getting hungry, but if he went into the Darband someone might spot him.

The barren mountains all round were like the world's end. Maybe places where it takes two days to make a phone call to Washington *are* the world's end.

Mechanically he checked Derieux's Colt. The silencer was heavy in his pocket. The clip was full, and the browned steel of the barrel flashed in the sun. Khadjar's people must be working their transmitter right now. The little plane standing quietly in a meadow, with a cargo of sudden death, just waiting for someone to swing the propeller.

What would happen if the Shah was killed? The Russians wouldn't let Khadjar set up a government without some sort of reaction. The Toudeh hadn't the power to express such a reaction on its own. There had to be direct intervention: Russian tanks could reach Teheran in four hours if they came

163

along the new strategic road to the north of El-brouz. After that it was anybody's guess what would happen. One thing was certain, though: the Iranian army wouldn't stop the Russians. No wonder the President had wanted to discuss this mission himself.

Four cops on motorcycles came out of the gate in a deep rumble of engines and stopped in the square, their machines throbbing gently. Malko sat up and turned the key in the ignition.

When the Shah came out of the gate he would be going relatively slowly. Malko wouldn't get another chance to stop him. He shifted gear and eased the Chevrolet forward until he was no more than fifty yards from the nearest of the motorcyclists. They didn't look at him. A car came out of the gate, a blue Chrysler sedan with two long aerials. It stopped behind the motorcycles.

Then he saw the Rolls, coming slowly down the driveway. He couldn't see inside because of the smoked glass, but there would be no one apart from the Shah and the Queen. The armored coachwork made bodyguards unnecessary.

The motorcyclists straddled their machines and moved slowly off, steering very straight with an air of fierce concentration. Malko let off the handbrake as the first went past. He must hit the Rolls from ahead, and before it could pick up speed.

It came clear of the gateway, and the Chevrolet bounded forward. No one turned. Then the second motorcyclist looked toward him, the goggles insect-like. He described a graceful curve across the road to block Malko's path. He wasn't worried, it was just a driver who had failed to recognize the Shah's car.

Malko still had time to surge forward and trap the Rolls. But he couldn't run this man down in cold blood—and he couldn't risk the shooting that would start immediately they suspected that something was wrong.

The Rolls whispered slowly by; Malko saw the Shah's profile dimly through the darkened glass, the Queen beside him. Three more cars, crammed with soldiers and policemen, brought up the rear.

It was too late. The procession swept with wailing sirens up the broad avenue.

Malko sighed. The motorcyclist waved him to drive on.

He headed back to Teheran because he couldn't think of anything else to do. It didn't matter now. The police would arrest him for stealing the car, he supposed. Two men at the side of the road gesticulated furiously, taking him for a taxi.

A honking of asthmatic horns behind him heralded a couple of coaches bulging with peasants on their way to the stadium. The bright blue sky sneered down. Millions were enjoying their lives at this moment. He studied a tiny moving speck in the sky, and felt a brotherly feeling toward it: they were both insignificant and purposeless. It grew larger and more distinct, and he slowed down, letting everyone pass him.

It was an airplane coming in to land at Mehrabad, flying always closer and lower in its steady shallow descent. Soon he could see the four underslung engines and then the identification marks—a Pan American Boeing 747. It turned in a huge flat curve, losing height and coming back toward the airfield. The big arrowhead tail showed him its blue world-circle and the aluminum fuselage gleamed in the sun.

"Jesus Christ Almighty," said Malko at the top of his voice, and braked as hard as he could. A taxi close behind missed him by something less than a hairsbreadth, and the driver screamed insultingly as he skidded past.

Malko stopped on the verge, and stared fixedly at the 747 as it went away to the south. He thought irrelevantly that Hildegarde might be on board.

There was an idea in his head that made his hair stand up on end. He could think of a hundred reasons why it wouldn't work. But it might.

He jammed the car into gear and took off with his rear wheels spinning. The avenue sloped down to the very center of Teheran, and there was little traffic. Crouched over the wheel, Malko had no time to see terrified pedestrians leaping for their lives. He had fifteen minutes to get to Mehrabad.

He overtook a long line of cars stopped at a traffic light, ran the red light and shot across under the nose of the cop in his little glass kiosk.

He was calm again now. He came on to the Mehrabad road alongside an Air France poster that said, 'Paris 5000 km'.

He was still five miles away, and he covered them in three and three quarter minutes. Luckily the road was empty. He forked right at the airport buildings to the entrance to the airfield proper. There was a gate leading to the runways, with a sentry; he just had time to spring aside as the Chevrolet went past him at seventy miles an hour.

Malko came out into the open directly opposite the parking circles. The 747 was there, the passengers forming solemn, slow-moving lines out of its dark belly. The fuel tankers were in position under the wings, and the luggage was being unloaded.

He pulled up just by the first-class gangway. The last passenger had just come down it and was trailing blearily away. Malko went up in two strides. After the bright sunlight he could see nothing inside the cabin. Then someone said, "Malko!" in a high voice and clung to his neck. Hildegarde. "What are you doing? How did you get here?"

"Where's the captain?" Malko demanded fiercely.

She stared at him. "What's the matter?"

"I can't explain now. Where's the captain?"

166

"He's in the cockpit, doing the landing checks. Wait a moment." Malko brushed past her and flung open a door marked 'crew only.'

The captain was leaning back in his seat, smoking and watching the co-pilot go through the rituals of debriefing. He thought Malko was a passenger come to have a look at the instruments, and smiled cheerfully and waved him in.

"Are you the captain?"

"That's me." He looked surprised, but went on smiling.

"I'm Malko Linge, I'm an officer of one United States Federal Agency, on special mission." The captain looked slightly more surprised and eyed Malko carefully.

Malko handed him the President's letter, and said, "Will you read this, please?" The captain's smile faded a bit more. Malko watched him. A fighter. Worn-looking for the little more than fifty years old he had to be to be still flying. Intelligent, a bit too frank. Obviously an old military flyer. Eyes as blue as the disc on the aircraft's tail.

He handed back the letter. "Mr. Linge, what can I do for you?"

Malko took a deep breath. "Take off. As soon as your passengers are clear."

"Take off." It was a statement.

"Take off. Just keep the flight crew, leave the hostesses. It could be risky."

The captain looked worried now. Malko thought, He thinks I'm out of my mind.

"Listen, Mr. Linge, do you know what you're saying? This plane's worth about six million bucks. I'm personally responsible for it to the company. You would have to have a very good reason. In fact I don't think any reason would be good enough. And in any case I can't take off without permission from Airport Control. I don't have the other companies' flight plans, and I don't plan to be chief witness at a public inquiry."

167

"If you asked the control tower for permission to take off what would they say?"

"They'd say no, of course."

"Then we'll have to do without it."

The captain shook his head patiently. "I can't do that. I don't know who you are, and I don't know what you want. I'd be risking my career, my life and probably the biggest airport disaster of all time, and for what?" Malko was about to speak, but he interrupted him. "Look, either you're crazy or you're serious, and you don't look crazy to me. But if I take this thing up, someone else has to take responsibility."

The man sounded half persuaded, but Malko could tell nothing from his face. The co-pilot was listening to them talk as he watched the needles on the fuel gauges steadily flickering over. The radio operator was writing figures on a printed card, and seemed not to hear.

Malko looked at his watch. It said five past two. "Captain, I'm going to give you the guarantee you want."

He unbuttoned his jacket and took the Colt out of his waistband, and unhurriedly screwed on the silencer. The three men watched him. None of them moved. "Now you have ten seconds to make up your mind, then I'll shoot you. You," to the co-pilot, "will have the same amount of time. Please believe me, I really regret having to take such extreme measures. I have no choice—and now neither have you."

There was a short silence. Then the captain said, "I guess we're persuaded. You'll be completely responsible for whatever happens, you understand. Now, will you please tell me what this is about?"

"Not till we're in the air."

"Okay, you're the boss. What happens now?"

"Do you have enough gas to stay up for an hour?"

"Sure."

168

"Okay, then stop refueling and get ready to take off."

He kept the gun in his hand, but he knew he wouldn't need it now.

"What do I tell Control?"

"Nothing."

"Okay. Frank, go down and tell the Shell guys to unhook, and warn the generator crew we're going to start up."

He turned back to Malko. "You're lucky the mechanics didn't find anything wrong with the engines. We should be ready for take-off in about five minutes."

The co-pilot had slipped outside, and Malko saw him talking to the ground crew. The fuel bunker crew disconnected their hoses and started to coil them neatly away. The man in charge of the generator was taking a little longer to convince; then he raised his thumbs in indication of agreement. Meanwhile a BOAC Boeing 707 taxied into the park and everyone lost interest in the Pam Am aircraft.

Malko watched the captain go steadily through his pre-flight checks. The two fuel tankers ground slowly away. The co-pilot came back on board and got rid of the cleaners. Then he bolted the heavy air-tight door as they left and walked forward to his seat. He went through his checklist and said, "Okay to take off, Cap."

"Okay. Start one."

The port outer engine whistled and roared.

"Start two."

Port inner.

"Three and four." Now the engines whistled in soft unison. Red and green warning lights winked on and off on the instrument panels. The generator crew climbed on to their little tractor and towed their apparatus away.

Malko put the pistol back in his waistband. He told himself he wouldn't look at his watch again until they were in the air. He looked at his watch. There was still time.

The radio crackled and said in English "Control to N-BHGE, what's happening? Why are you starting engines?"

The Captain picked up the microphone. "N-BHGE to Control, I am hijacked—no more in control of plane. I have to take off."

The crackling started again, then Control said, "Permission not granted."

"Sorry, but I am at gunpoint."

Radio out.

The captain operated flaps and ailerons, released the brakes and eased the throttles open. The heavy Boeing rolled gently forward parallel with the line of concrete buildings.

"You hear that?" the captain said to Malko. "He told us not to take off."

"I heard. But they can't act soon enough to stop us."

The Boeing picked up speed. The airport buildings shrank behind them. Malko stood behind the captain, staring at the sharp-perspective runway ahead. The crackling of the radio ripped the air like paper.

"Kill that noise, will you?" Malko said.

The radio operator threw a switch and the crackling stopped. The Boeing arrived at the intersection with the take-off runway. The captain braked, and when the plane was still, turned to face Malko. "What now?"

"Presumably you can steer without a fixed objective? Okay, steer forty-five degrees and keep going."

The captain hauled back his four throttle-levers. The aircraft began to tremble, straining against the brakes. The radio operator suddenly said, "Look, captain, on the runway." Malko and the captain stared at the end of the runway. A jeep was coming toward the plane. The dust said it was in a hurry.

Control must have got nervous about the hijacking.

Malko said, "You've still got time." He hoped his voice sounded confident.

The captain shook his head. "He's going pretty fast."

"Then you'll have to take off early." He pulled out the Colt again and held it loosely at his side. This was a bad time to be indecisive.

The engine noise grew louder, and the plane seemed to lean forward. The jeep was still tiny, but they were closing with it fast.

"We're going to hit it," said the captain.

"Keep going."

It was in the middle of the runway now. Malko could see the men in it waving their arms, and their mouths silently working. "If they stay in the middle of the runway we'll all be killed," the captain shouted.

"Keep going."

The 747 trembled and yawed slightly on the wide concrete. The jeep was barely half a mile away.

Malko said, "How much more to take off?"

"Maybe six hundred yards."

They were going to hit the jeep. The men in it thought they were going to stop, just like that. It didn't change course. The engines howled, and Malko's guts contracted into a tight small knot.

The captain pulled back the control column with both hands. The nose of the 747 lifted gracefully and the jeep slid under the fuselage and away behind the tail. They were tilted at a ladder-steep angle. The airfield turned into a bedspread, and then a bright green and yellowish-grey handkerchief.

Malko took another deep breath. The captain and co-pilot were busy with their instruments and controls, raising the under-carriages and trimming the flaps, throttling the engines back to cruising speed. Level with the first clouds they started to straighten.

The captain turned to Malko. "You're lucky we have no payload; I've never taken off with so short a run before. The radar will pick us up pretty well immediately, we'll have fighters on our tail soon."

"They won't shoot down a hijacked American civil aircraft."

"They won't have to, they can force us down by buzzing us."

"Plenty can happen between now and then."

The captain swivelled his seat round and scratched his neck, screwing up his eyes. "What *is* going to happen between now and then? I never was hijacked before."

"What's the lowest altitude you can fly at?"

"Eight, maybe six hundred feet. That's with flaps right down. Damn dangerous: I wouldn't want to play that sort of game for too long at a time."

"How fast would you have to be going?"

"Two hundred plus."

"Do you have any maneuverability at that sort of speed?"

"Twenty-degree flat turns is about the limit."

"I see. Captain, were you in the war?"

"Sure. Why?"

"Where?"

"Europe. I was flying bombers."

"Remember the V–1s—the German flying bombs?"

"Sure."

"Do you remember how the English fighter-pilots stopped them when they got through the anti-aircraft screen?"

"Yes, they got alongside and tipped the things over with their wingtips; so what? Look, what the hell are you getting at? The war's been over a long time, there aren't any flying bombs in Iran, and this isn't a fighter, it's a goddam hundred-and-eighty-ton luxury liner."

172

"That's wrong, wrong and wrong," said Malko. "At least, there are a couple of guys here that don't know about the war being over; there *are* flying bombs in Iran—at least one that I know of; and this Zeppelin just got promoted." The captain tried to decide whether to be angry or simply amazed and while he was making up his mind Malko explained about the assassination. "We can't shoot the thing down, so we'll have to knock it down."

"That's nice. That's easy. All you want is miracles," the captain said bitterly.

"I didn't say it was easy, I just say we don't have any choice.

"Anyway," Malko added, "we won't have to knock it down—flying very close will be enough. I've noticed these engines leave something like a tornado behind them."

"*You* don't have any choice. Okay, so where's this thing going to be taking off from?"

"Unfortunately that's a detail I don't know; but it has to be near the stadium, on account of having to stay in range of the radio control. The stadium's north of Teheran, between the town and the mountains. So it has to be either east or west. From what I know of the country east is a better bet."

They were flying at five thousand feet above the city. The sky was very clear, except for a little cumulus, and they could see the streets like a boardgame precisely picked out below.

"We don't have much time," Malko said. "Head for the stadium and lose some altitude, and we'll see how it pans out."

The Boeing tipped and slid gradually down to fifteen hundred feet. They could see the ground in watchmaker detail. The stadium swam into vision and they slid slowly over it with the flaps down. Malko could see the saluting base and the Shah standing on it. A lot of gymnasts were doing some sort of unison routine on the grass, stamping and windmilling their white-clad arms and legs. Everything looked normal. No one looked up. Long-distance airliners often did a circuit of the town before putting down in Mehrabad.

"Go back the way we came and set a course east," said Malko, guessing. The plane leaned over and lost more altitude. When they passed over the stadium this time all the spectators looked up as the noise of the engines drowned out the band. Malko stared down at the desert trying to see something unusual, but it stretched out of sight unvarying except for the ocher spots of sun-baked mud buildings.

The town was already a long way behind. Malko opened his mouth to say "Turn," but the co-pilot pointed and said, "Down there, to the right," and Malko twisted his neck and saw a little bright yellow airplane taxiing slowly along in the middle of the desert.

"That must be it," he said, but the Boeing was already a long way past. With enormous care the pilot bent it into an impossibly tight turn. The wingtip seemed almost to touch the ground. Then they straightened up and flew back toward the stadium at about a thousand feet. They were back at the improvised runway in the desert in two minutes but it was empty except for a stationary car and a pile of empty gasoline drums.

They flew for two or three minutes, staring at the white sunlight coming off the ground, and then the co-pilot shouted again, and the yellow insect was creeping in front of them and a good deal lower. It was heading straight for the stadium.

"We're going over it," muttered the captain.

"So go down," Malko said.

"I was afraid you'd say that," the captain said. The Boeing sank like a heavy flat fish, the flaps opened wider and the engines throttled back and back. A hideous screeching, whistling sound filled the cabin; Malko flinched, but the captain just said, "Alarm siren. We're flying too low and too slow; in case you didn't notice."

The yellow plane was now about two hundred yards behind the 747.

The second pilot said, "We're going to look pretty smart if it's some Sunday driver." But Malko just said, "Look." They were slightly over the other aircraft and could see into the cockpit. It was empty.

The captain and Malko looked at each other at the same time and didn't say anything. The yellow plane would be at the stadium in about three minutes.

The captain juggled his control column as though he were trying to get it exactly vertical but it kept slipping, and somehow he reduced the distance between the two planes. He throttled back even more, and the whole fuselage started to tremble. The yellow plane was coming closer and closer. Malko saw the white open-mouthed faces of a group of herdsmen three hundred feet below.

The Boeing was pitching and rolling, and Malko saw the captain's knuckles whiten on the controls. Suddenly, the small yellow plane started rolling, shaking—caught on the trail of the big 747. Then it dived to the ground. Then there was a deafening roar and Malko was thrown brutally against the bulkhead by a terrific acceleration. The captain had quickly wagged the whole plane, and then gone full throttle all the way. The Boeing stood on its engines as they howled at take-off power.

Malko, on all fours in the cockpit, struggled to get up, when the whole plane was batted like a tennis ball by an immense huff of wind. As he careened back down the floor there was a noise like thunder, and he forgot the new bump on his head.

He scrambled weakly to his feet and staggered back into the flight-deck. Through the left-hand windows he saw a great tower of black smoke climbing out of the desert half a mile away.

That was all they saw, as they swept back across the stadium at a hundred feet. Malko could clearly see the faces of the Shah and the people around him on the saluting platform. They looked surprised and frightened.

Finally the captain gained a little height. He turned to Malko, grinned and said, "Never doubt a man with a gun. What now?"

"Home. And get back into radio contact."

"And not a moment too soon. Look." Six little specks on the horizon turned into Phantoms of the Iranian Air Force. They surrounded the Boeing like seagulls around a transatlantic liner and signalled it to land.

Malko said to the captain, "Call Control and tell them that we've just prevented an assassination attempt, and that we'll only leave the plane under the personal protection of the U.S. Ambassador. Someone'll have to bring him from the stadium."

"You're kidding. After what I've been through I expect bouquets and brass bands. We're heroes now, remember?"

Malko did his world-weary, when-you've-seen-what-I've-seen smile. "Not necessarily. That bomb was arranged by General Khadjar, whom you may have heard of. Head of the Secret Police? A guy with a lot of pull. He'd be pretty pleased to have an opportunity to get me off his back."

Undercarriage down. Flaps. A hundred feet, fifty feet, crash and squeal of tires, then they were rolling down the runway, past the black rubber-stains of other landings. It was three fourteen.

The radio blared and crackled angrily. Two jeeps full of soldiers came in front of the plane and escorted it into the parking area, presumably in case the pilot should take it into his head to keep going out on to the main road to Teheran. He parked it docilely in the circle he had left an hour before. The gangways were rolled into place against the doors, but the doors stayed shut. The radio became indignant, then shrill and finally abusive. A small group of Pan Am staff came and stared in a worried way at the mutinous liner. No one told them anything.

Soldiers with submachine-guns surrounded the aircraft, but none of them tried to get in.

In the cockpit Malko and the crew sat and waited, smoking and not saying anything.

Finally a long black Cadillac with the Stars and Stripes fluttering from a little mast on one wing came on to the field, stopped at the foot of the first-class gangway and disgorged Ambassador Kilroy.

Malko didn't smile.

CHAPTER THIRTEEN

The Ambassador saw the silenced pistol stuck in Malko's waistband and winced. Malko didn't let him speak. "Mr. Ambassador," he said politely, "would you kindly take me to your embassy? Under your personal protection, please; I have to talk with the White House."

There seemed to be things the Ambassador wanted to say, but Malko cut him off again. "As representative here of the American government you will place General Schalberg under arrest and confine him to the embassy. And you will arrange for me to see the Shah at once. I think you ought to know that there has been an unsuccessful assassination attempt by members of our own agencies and of certain of the Iranian military services. As the crew of this airplane will bear witness.

"Now let's go. And try not to forget that you're protected by diplomatic immunity."

Kilroy shook his head like a diver surfacing. "Mr. Linge," he began, but Malko took him by the elbow in a friendly way and said: "Listen, right now you could get off with a transfer to some nice quiet mission where life won't be too difficult, but if you say any more you'll really be in trouble."

He was making it all up as he went along, but Kilroy seemed to be silenced. Malko followed him down the gangway, his hand on the butt of the pistol. No one else moved. Malko's face was expressionless, but when he was safely in the back seat of the Cadillac he permitted himself a small smile, which he took care to hide from the Ambassador.

The limousine carved silently through the town and wound squealing into the embassy courtyard. They got out and Kilroy led the way into his office. Malko sat behind his desk under the American flags and eagle and composed a message. "Would you have this telexed as soon as possible, please; and send for General Schalberg."

The Ambassador took the piece of paper and left the room without answering. He came back in ten minutes and said, "The general isn't in the embassy. I've ordered the Marines to bring him here as soon as he arrives."

"Thank you," said Malko. "I am going to rest for little while. There'll be a reply to the telex. You wake me when it comes. And meanwhile you might arrange the meeting with the Shah." The Ambassador looked prim and disapproving while Malko took off his shoes, laid the Colt down beside him and stretched out on the black leather upholstery. Five minutes later he was asleep.

"Your Highness. Your Highness." Malko groaned, and reluctantly climbed out of his dream. He liked being called by his title, but it had been a good dream. The Ambassador was bending over him with a sheet of telex paper. Malko sat up and took it. It was Washington's reply, and it told him why Kilroy was acting like a high-class valet. He was ordered to place himself entirely, "repeat entirely," at Malko's disposal, and it was signed by the head of the State Department.

"His Majesty's waiting for us at the palace. It's a special audience."

A faint smile spread over Malko's face. Together at last. "Let's go, then," he said, lacing his shoes. "Any news of Schalberg?"

Kilroy shook his head.

The Cadillac waited for them in the courtyard like a shiny stranded dolphin. Malko stared at the carpet and smiled, and Kilroy looked nervously out of the window as the car whispered through the city. When they arrived a general of the Imperial Guard hurried forward to meet them.

"General Nessari," muttered Kilroy. "Commander of all the Shah's personal troops."

They walked behind the Iranian general across the park to the marble palace. All the way there were heavily-built sentries at five-yard intervals, with submachine-guns and faces of stone. Two officers stood in attitudes of casual watchfulness outside the Shah's door. They showed Kilroy and Malko in, announced them and left.

It was an unassuming room, little more than an office, except for the desk, which was inlaid all over with mother-of-pearl, with the inevitable red telephone sitting on it.

"Please sit down, gentlemen," said the Shah. He seemed like a nice guy. Intelligent, a bit cynical. Carefully-tended graying hair. Two big men in tight suits stood unobtrusively in a dark corner.

Kilroy introduced Malko. The Shah nodded and said, "It seems you've saved my life. I owe you a debt of thanks." He spoke precisely, like a man who learns foreign languages for a purpose rather than for pleasure. Malko bowed politely and said nothing.

The Shah said, "I would like you to tell me what happened."

"Everything?"

"Certainly."

He told the whole story, omitting nothing. The Shah's eyebrows slid up a little when Malko went into the Tania episodes, but he'd asked for everything. As the story progressed the Ambassador sank deeper and more miserably into his chair. The Shah listened, asked questions from time to time and took notes. Once he scribbled on a scrap of paper and gave it to one of his bodyguards, who nodded and went softly out of the room.

By the time Malko had finished night had fallen

and a servant had come to light the lamps and drift away again. The Shah sat in silence for a little while. Then he said, "Mr. Linge, I believe you. I have sent for General Khadjar to ask him some questions. If he is guilty of these things a military tribunal will condemn him. But what you have said confirms information from other sources." He smiled. "No man is a prophet in his own country, Mr. Linge. Mr. Kilroy, you will deal with General Schalberg, I take it?"

Kilroy nodded energetically, eager to be back in someone's good favor.

The Shah rose and shook hands. The audience was over. Outside, Kilroy said grudgingly, "He seemed quite pleased. You have an unusually good memory, Mr. Linge."

"I just hope he'll be able to catch up with the generals, they've still got some life left in them. Mr. Ambassador, would you mind taking me back to my hotel? I need a shower."

The Cadillac climbed easily up the hill to the Hilton. As they arrived they were overtaken by a blue Chrysler, traveling fast. Its nose dipped as it pulled up sharply in front of the hotel entrance, and General Nessari leaped out. He hurried in ahead of Malko and Kilroy and went up to the reception desk. The clerk listened and nodded earnestly. When Malko went to get his key the manager bowed until he seemed about to snap in two.

Malko said goodbye to Kilroy and went upstairs. He plunged into a shower, put on a clean shirt and suit, doused himself in *eau de cologne* and stepped out into the corridor.

And stepped immediately back again, as he saw two soldiers with submachine-guns standing outside the door. He hadn't thought Khadjar's people would come for him in the hotel. He waited, but they didn't come into the room. He listened, but there was no sound. He shrugged and strode out

181

again. They sprang to attention and clicked their heels. He frowned in astonishment. Then he shrugged again and walked to the elevator. The attendant shot him to the ground floor before he could say where he was going, ignoring the impatiently winking lights of all the other floors on the way down.

He stepped rather breathlessly out of the elevator, and the manager rushed up to him, bowing in quick tempo. "You are His Majesty's guest this evening, Your Highness, and he has asked us to ensure that you have every comfort. Would you like to dine in a private room?"

Malko said no, he'd rather sit in the restaurant with the peasantry. They gave him a table by the window. No menu was brought. Instead the *maître d'hôtel* appeared and ceremoniously placed a small opaque jar on the table in front of him.

"A present from His Majesty," he murmured. "White caviar. Extremely rare."

Malko had never seen it before. He tried a tentative spoonful: it tasted exactly the same as ordinary black Beluga. Still, the Shah wasted no time in showing his gratitude. As he finished his third piece of toast, Malko noticed two tough-looking men sitting quietly at a small table behind his left shoulder. They looked about as unobtrusive as the two soldiers in the corridor. There must be at least a tank outside. The waiter brought a delicious shashlik but he was full of caviar and fatigue, and he scarcely touched it. He was suddenly depressed and let down. He had called Hildegarde's room, but there was no reply. Just this evening he needed a little pleasant relaxation.

After the Turkish coffee he went to bed. He dragged his clothes off and fell onto the spread, already asleep.

The telephone woke him. He flailed sluggishly around and discovered the receiver. Then he found his ear, and brought them together.

"This is Kilroy," said the Ambassador. "Wake up, old man, I've got news for you."

"The Russians are attacking?" said Malko. He'd been awakened by the telephone too often recently.

"That isn't funny," the Ambassador said coldly. "No, General Khadjar was nearly arrested this morning."

"This morning? What's the time?"

"Mid-day. He shot the two officers who came to arrest him and went underground in, believe it or not, the vault of the Bank Melli where they keep the treasure that backs the rial."

"Alone?"

Kilroy hesitated. "Unfortunately not. Schalberg's with him, plus two of our people and Khadjar's adjutant. All armed. The police have sealed off the bank, but they're going to be hard to pry out. That's a real strong-room, and no mistake. I'm going there now, do you want to meet me there?"

"I'll be with you as soon as I can get some clothes on."

For once he skipped the shower, made do with a clean shirt and hurried out into the corridor without his gun. There was no need for it, though; the two strong-men of the night before sprang up from a seat in the lobby and tagged on behind him. At the entrance, a third man came up to him. "The car's over here, Mr. Linge."

It was a pale blue Chrysler, without a license, and with a chauffeur in uniform. He got in the back, and the heavies piled in the front.

"Bank Melli," Malko ordered, but the Chrysler had already shot away, and he had to hang on to the strap to hold himself in the wide seat. The chauffeur pressed a switch and started a siren. Just like cops in America, Malko thought nostalgically.

The twenty-minute journey took them just ten. They pulled up in front of a military roadblock, about a hundred yards short of the bank. Malko got out and Kilroy rushed over to him.

"Glad you got here, the Shah wants a word with you."

"Where?"

"Over there, in his car. He came here himself to see the arrests made. He's waiting for you."

The gray Rolls was parked opposite the bank, surrounded by troops.

"How long has this been going on?" Malko asked as they walked over.

"Nearly three hours now. And it could go on a good deal longer. The vault's impregnable, underground, armor-plated, everything. The door's steel, three feet thick."

The Shah was sitting in the back of the car, smoking and looking bored. He signaled to Malko to get in. "You were absolutely right, Mr. Linge," he said by way of greeting. "General Khadjar has betrayed my confidence. You have done my country a great service," the Shah went on, "and I shall make it known in the appropriate quarters." He was thoughtful for a moment. "You have my personal thanks too, Mr. Linge, and I shall express them more fully in due course." He held out his hand. "And now I must go back to the palace. I have other things to do. Good morning, Mr. Linge."

"But—but what about the generals?" Malko couldn't help asking.

The Shah smiled briefly. "That problem has been solved already, in the best interests of all concerned."

Malko got out and swung the heavy door shut with a soft click, then went back to where Kilroy was standing. The Rolls crept silently away. Soon the soldiers started to form up, also preparing to leave.

"What's going on?" Kilroy asked.

"I don't know. The Shah's very cool. You'd think he wasn't interested in this thing any more. Look." All around them the soldiers and police were packing up. Soon they were alone except for four policemen standing on guard outside the building that contained the treasure room.

Kilroy and Malko went over to it and were permitted to approach the door. Pinned to it was a card, on which was written, in Persian and English, "Closed for repairs."

As he strolled away in utter perplexity, Malko thought of Derieux. The poor chap must still be tucked away in his burrow. He exchanged cars with Kilroy; no point in putting the Shah's people on to the old doctor.

Even with his memory he had trouble finding the place. He knocked and the old woman let him in. The doctor wasn't there. He moved the table and opened the trapdoor. The ladder was in place.

He dropped into the lower room and the silencer of the Colt pressed against his cheek. Derieux smiled and put the gun down. "You should have said something; I was just about to shoot you. What's new?"

"Nothing much," said Malko, sitting on the bed. "We're just national heroes, that's all." He brought him up to date.

Derieux grinned like a cat. "Virtue rewarded at last. That's the kind of service the Shah doesn't forget. Boy, things are going to get nothing but better."

Malko went to get the driver. Between them they got Derieux up the ladder and out to the car. Derieux muttered something about people who steal great big limousines, and sat back luxuriously.

"I wonder what the Shah's got lined up for Schalberg and Khadjar?"

"Maybe he's going to starve them to death."

"No, he'd've left troops in case they got out."

The car went slowly back up Lalehzar Street. Malko saw a news vendor waving a special edition of the *Teheran Journal*. He dropped the window and called him over.

There was just one headline:

General Khadjar, head of Iranian Security, accompanied by the American General Schalberg and several colleagues, accidentally drowned today during a visit to the treasure room of the bank.

The article below explained that in the course of a demonstration of the security system, the doors had been accidentally closed and the room flooded, these being devices to prevent the escape of thieves. Those responsible for this shocking negligence would be severely dealt with.

There followed a long obituary extolling the merits of the two generals. The Shah had expressed his personal condolences to the widows, and General Schalberg was posthumously decorated with the Zolfanaghar (first class), the highest Persian honor. General Khadjar unfortunately could receive no such honor, as he already had them all.

The funeral had been fixed for the next day, which was proclaimed a holiday and day of national mourning. The Shah would of course be presiding over the funeral rites himself.

"That's very smart of him," Derieux commented. "Drowned like rats and buried like princes. The old Shah knows how to do things. They wouldn't have done as much for him."

Malko dropped Derieux at his home and went back to the hotel. He still had a great deal to do.

His guards were still there, clicking their heels. And as he came into the room his telephone was ringing, and it was Tania. "I'm so glad you got away safely," she chattered. "You know, you owe that partly to me. Wasn't it a pity about Teymour? Such a good-looking man."

Malko was making an odd choking noise, and didn't say anything, so she went on, "What about

186

our trip to Karaj? The offer's still open. I'll be free tomorrow because of the holiday."

Malko had an entertaining idea. "Fine," he said, "come and pick me up tomorrow. I'll have a surprise for you."

"Okay," said Tania, pleased. "See you tomorrow. I'll make myself specially beautiful for you."

Malko hung up, smiling.

The water of Lake Karaj was as smooth as silk. The huge rocky slopes surrounding it made it seem very small. The crisp mountain air, the blue sky, the light breeze, made one want to run and swim.

"Who's going to make lunch?" Malko asked maliciously. "I could eat a horse."

"I'm not much good at cooking." Hildegarde, pouting, poured into sky-blue trousers and a cashmere sweater.

Tania said nothing, and went to the trunk of the car to get the picnic basket. Malko watched her, suppressing the urge to laugh hysterically, as he remembered her face when she'd arrived an hour earlier and found him with Hildegarde in tow.

Their romantic weekend wasn't going quite as planned. There were two rooms in Tania's little house by the lake: hers and theirs.

She pushed out her bosom as she passed in front of him, and brushed him lightly with her hip, and for an instant he regretted the trick. But then, Hildegarde would be leaving the next day, and Tania would be staying.

She'd only love him more.

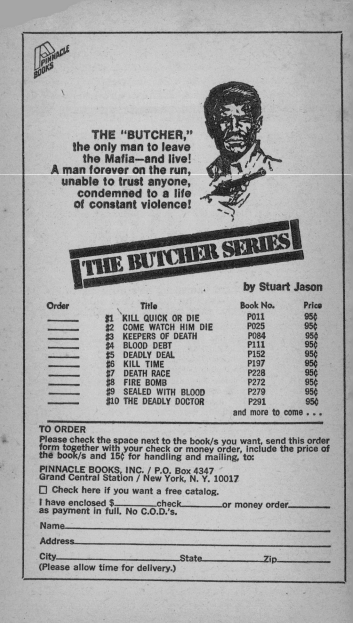